THE S1
THE

MW01255092

It seemed like a remarkable lucky streak to be sure, but when Allan Commager went on an unprecedented fifteen-minute winning session at the craps tables, it set off an unexpected chain of events. He soon found himself at the house of someone he barely knew, surrounded by strange people, being subjected to parlor room experiments of the mind. But to a secret society known as "the Guides," it was no trickery. And when Commager's consciousness revived several hours later, he found himself sitting in front of a fish tank staring into its dark waters. It was then he knew that something was terribly wrong. Soon the mental powers of outside forces turned Commager's world upside. There was something about his brain that caused them great concern—that caused them to fear him!

FOR A COMPLETE SECOND NOVEL, TURN TO PAGE 105

CAST OF CHARACTERS

ALAN COMMAGER
It was a big blank spot in his memory that made Alan realize there was something different about himself—about his brain.

PARLAY
She was strangely elusive. A truly beautiful yet mysterious woman—but extremely dangerous in her own "thoughtful" way.

JEAN BOHART
This genial, attractive lady was one of Commager's best friends. But did she feel more than friendship?

LEX BARTHOLD
He didn't seem to be anything more than a muscle-beach-type kid—until he showed up one night with a gun in his hand.

WILSON KNOX
Was he just some sort of eccentric religious kook, or perhaps something more sinister?

IRA BOHART
He had a penchant for the metaphysical unknown that could drive his wife and friends a little crazy at times.

ELAINE LOVELOCK
She appeared to be an old, heavy-set, not-to-attractive nurse. But her mind held the darkest secret of Commager's past.

THE TIES
OF EARTH

By
JAMES H. SCHMITZ

ARMCHAIR FICTION
PO Box 4369, Medford, Oregon   97501-0168

CHAPTER ONE

THE HAWKES residence lay in a back area of Beverly Hills, south of Wilshire and west of La Brea. It was a big house for that neighborhood, a corner house set back from the street on both sides and screened by trellises, walls and the flanks of a large garage.

"That's the number," Jean Bohart said, "but don't stop. Drive on at least a block..."

Alan Commager pointed out that there was parking space right in front of the house.

"I know," Jean agreed nervously, "but if we park there, somebody inside the house would notice us and that would spoil the main purpose of our trip."

"You mean," said Commager as he drove on obediently, "they'll fold the black altar out of sight, drop the remains of the sacrificed virgin through a trap door and hose out the blood, while we're stumbling across the dichondra? I thought we were expected."

"We're not expected till ten-thirty," Jean said. "Ira didn't exactly make a point of it, but he mentioned they'd be doing other work till shortly after ten."

"Then I come on with the dice, eh? By the way, I didn't bring any along. Would these Guides keep sordid little items like that around?"

"It isn't going to be a crap game, silly," Jean informed him. "I told you Ira thinks these people can tell whether you were just lucky last week or whether you've developed some sort of special ability. They'll test you—somehow."

COMMAGER looked down at her curiously. Jean was a slim blonde who could look crisp as chilled lettuce after an afternoon of smashing tennis matches followed by an hour of diving practice off the high board. She wasn't intellectually inclined, but, understandably, Ira Bohart had never seemed to mind that. Neither did Commager. However, she seemed disturbed now.

"Are you beginning to get interested in that sort of thing yourself?" he inquired lightly.

"No," she said. "I'm just worried about that husband of mine. Honestly, Alan, this is as bad a metaphysical binge as he's ever been on! And some of those exercises he was showing me yesterday sort of scared me. If they do something like that tonight, I'd like to know what you think of it."

"It's just somebody else on the trail of the Bohart stocks and bonds, Jeannie! Ira will get disillusioned again before any harm is done. You know that, Jeannie."

"That's what I keep telling myself," Jean agreed unhappily. "But this time—"

Commager shook his head, parked the car and let her out, a block and a half from the Hawkes home. "Did you try any of those exercises yourself?"

"I'm not that loony," Jean said briefly. "Anyway, Ira advised me not to."

They walked back to the house in brooding silence. Between them, they'd seen Ira through a bout of Buddhism and successive experiences with three psychological fringe groups, in relentless pursuit of some form of control of the Higher Mind. After each such period, he would revert for a while to despondent normalcy.

Four years ago, it had seemed rather amusing to Commager, because then it had been Lona Commager and Ira Bohart who went questing after the Inexpressible together, while Alan Commager and Jean Bohart went sea-fishing or skin-diving off Catalina. But then Lona had died and the Inexpressible stopped being a source of amusement. Sometimes Ira bored Commager to death these days. But he still liked Jean.

"WHY PICK on me to expose these rascals anyway?" he asked as they came in sight of the house. "I may have surprised the boys at Las Vegas last week, but I couldn't tell a psychic phenomenon from a ringing in my ears."

She patted his arm. "That may be true, but you do intimidate people," she explained.

"Shucks..." Commager said modestly. It was true, though; he did. "So I'm to sit there and glare at them?"

"That's the idea. Just let them know you see through their little tricks and I'll bet they lose interest in Ira before the evening's out! Of course, you don't have to put it on too thick..."

Their host, Herbert Hawkes, for one, didn't look like a man who'd be easy to intimidate. He was as big as Commager himself and about the same age; an ex-football player, it turned out. He and Commager exchanging crushing hand-grips and soft smiles, as big men will, and released each other with mutual respect.

Ira, who didn't seem any more gaunt and haggard than usual, had appeared a little startled by their entry, possibly because they were early, but more likely, Commager thought, because of a girl who had coiled herself becomingly on the couch very close to Ira.

At first glance, this siren seemed no more than seventeen—a slender, brown-skinned creature in an afternoon dress the exact shade of her skin—but by the time they were being introduced, Commager had added twelve years to her probable age.

She was Ruth MacDonald, she told him, secretary of the Parapsychological Group of Long Beach. Had he heard of it? He said it sounded familiar, which was untrue, but it seemed to please Miss MacDonald.

The only other person present, a fifty-odd, graying teddy bear of a man with very thick eyebrows, announced he was the Reverend Wilson Knox, president of the Temple of Antique Christianity. The Reverend, Commager realized, was pretty well plastered, though there was no liquor in sight.

THEIR INTERESTS might be unusual, but they hardly seemed sinister. Commager was practically certain he could identify Herbert Hawkes as the owner of one of the biggest downtown automobile agencies, which made him an unlikely sort of man to be a member of a group called the Guides. It was Hawkes's own affair, but it promised to make the evening more interesting than Commager had expected.

"Were we interrupting anything?" he inquired, looking around benevolently.

Ira cleared his throat. "Well, as a matter of fact, Alan, we were conducting a series of experiments with me as the guinea pig at the moment. Rather interesting actually—" He seemed a trifle nervous.

Commager avoided Jean's glance. "Why not just continue?"

"We can't," the Reverend Knox informed him solemnly. "Our high priestess was called to the telephone a few minutes ago. We must wait until she returns."

Ira explained hurriedly, "Mr. Knox is talking about Paylar. She's connected with the new group I'm interested in, the Guides. I suppose Jean told you about that?"

"A little." Commager waved his hand around. "But I thought you people were the Guides."

Hawkes smiled.

Wilson Knox looked startled. "Goodness, no, Mr. Commager! Though as a matter of fact..." He glanced somewhat warily at his two companions. "...if someone here were a Guide, that person would be the only one who knew it! And, of course, Paylar. That's right, isn't it, Ruth?"

Miss MacDonald nodded and looked bored.

Jean said to Ira, "All I really told Alan was that some friends of yours would like to experiment with—well, whatever you think he was using in that craps game last week." She smiled brightly at the group. "Mr. Commager actually won eleven hundred dollars in fifteen minutes of playing!"

"Ah, anybody could if they kept the dice for fifteen minutes," Commager said airily. "Question of mind over matter, you know."

"Eleven hundred dollars? Phenomenal!" Wilson Knox came wide-awake. "And may I ask, sir, whether you employ your powers as a professional gambler?"

Commager replied no, that professionally he was a collector, importer, wholesaler and retailer of tropical fish. Which was, as it happened, the truth, but the Reverend looked suspicious.

A DOOR opened then and two other people came in. One was a handsome though sullen-faced young man whose white-blond hair had been trimmed into a butch haircut. He was deeply tanned, wore a tee shirt, white slacks, sneakers and looked generally as if he would be at home on Muscle Beach.

The other one had to be Paylar: a genuine Guide or, at least, a direct connection to them. She was downright cute in a slender, dark way. She might be in her early twenties...

But for a moment, as Commager stood up to be introduced, he had the confused impression that jungles and deserts and auroras mirrored in ice-flows had come walking into the room with her.

Well, well, he thought. Along with Hawkes, here was another real personality.

They didn't continue with the experiments on Ira. Wilson Knox reported Commager's feat in Las Vegas to Paylar, who seemed to know all about it, and then went bumbling on into a series of anecdotes about other dice manipulators he had known or heard about.

Except for the Boharts, the others listened with varying expressions of polite boredom. But Ira seemed genuinely fascinated by the subject and kept glancing at Commager, to see how he was taking it. Jean became argumentative.

"Nobody can really prove that anyone has such abilities!" she stated decisively. "Ira's been working around with this sort of thing for years and he's never shown me anything that couldn't have been a coincidence"

Ira grinned apologetically. Wilson Knox sent a quick glance toward Paylar, who had settled herself in an armchair to Commager's left. The Reverend, Commager thought, seemed both miffed and curiously apprehensive.

Commager's own interest in the group became suddenly more lively.

"There are people in this world today, my dear young lady," Wilson Knox was telling Jean, "who control the Secret Powers of the Universe..."

Jean sighed. "When Ira tells me something like that, I always want to know why we don't hear what these mysterious people are doing."

WILSON KNOX glanced at Paylar again. And this time, Commager decided, there was no question about it: the odd little man seemed genuinely alarmed. The bushy eyebrows were working in unconcealed agitation.

"We must consider," he told Jean helplessly, "that such people have their reasons for not revealing their abilities."

"Hm!" sniffed Jean.

Commager laughed. "Mrs. Bohart has a point there, you know," he said to Paylar. "I understand the Guides imply they can, at any rate, train people to develop extrasensory abilities. Would you say they can produce some tangible proof for that claim?"

"Sometimes," she said. "With some people." She looked a little tired of the subject, as if it were something she had heard discussed often, as she probably had, so Commager was surprised when she added in the same tone, "I could, I think, produce such proofs very easily for you, Mr. Commager. To your own satisfaction, at least."

As she turned to look at him, her dark elfin face sober and confident, Commager was aware of a sudden stillness in the room. Wilson Knox started what seemed to be a protesting gesture and subsided again. And Jean was frowning, as if she had just discovered an unexpected uncertainty in herself.

"It's a fair offer," Commager acknowledged. "If you're suggesting an experiment, I'll be glad to cooperate."

For a moment, he saw something almost like compassion in the serious young face that studied him. Then Paylar turned to the others. "Would you arrange the lighting in the usual way? Mr. Commager, I should like you to sit here."

It was what they had come here for, Commager thought. Hawkes and the blond young man, whose name was Lex Barthold, went about the room adjusting the lights. Commager had a strong impression that Jean now would just as soon keep the experiment from being carried out, if she could think of a good enough reason.

But the experiment would be a flop anyway. No such half-mystical parlor games had worked on Commager since Lana had died.

CHAPTER TWO

IN COMMAGER'S tropical fish store on Wilshire Boulevard, there were display tanks that were laid out with the casual stateliness of an English park and others that had the formal delicacy of a Chinese garden or that appeared to copy, in fantastic miniature detail, sections of some dreamland salt-water reef. These were the designs of two artistically minded girls who managed the store for Commager and they were often expensively duplicated by artists themselves in the homes of the shop's less talented patrons.

But the tanks that most interested Commager were the big ones in the back of the store, partitioned off from the plate-glass windows and the displays that faced the boulevard. Here fish and plants were bred, raised and stocked without regard for art, and the effect, when you sat down to watch them for a while, was that of being in the center of a secret, green-lit jungle out of which God knew what might presently come soaring, wriggling or crawling at you.

It wasn't a bad way, in Commager's opinion, to pass a few hours at night, when you didn't happen to be in a mood either for sleep or human company. In his case, that might happen once or twice a week, or perhaps less than once a month. When it happened more often, it was time to get organized for another one of those trips that would wind up at some warm and improbable point on the big globe of Earth, where people were waiting to help Commager fill his transport tanks with brightly colored little water-creatures—

which, rather surprisingly, provided him with a very good income.

It was a pattern he had followed for most of the second half of his thirty-four years, the only two interruptions having been the second world war and the nineteen months he'd been married to Lana.

It was odd, he thought, that he'd never found anything more important to do with his life than that, but the personal games he could watch people play didn't seem to be even as interesting as the one he'd chosen for himself.

Also, he went on thinking half-seriously, if you got right down to it, probably all the important elements of life were contained right inside the big tank he was observing at the moment, so that if he could really understand what was going on in there, brightly and stealthily among the green underwater thickets, he might know all that could be known about the entire Universe.

Considered in that light, the tank became as fascinating as a stage play in a foreign language, in which the actors wore the bright masks of magic and played games that weren't so very unlike those being played by human beings. But any real understanding of the purpose of the play, human or otherwise, always had seemed a little beyond Commager's reach.

HE YAWNED and shifted position in the chair he had pulled up for himself. Perhaps he was simply a bit more stupid than most. But there was a fretting feeling that this game playing, whether on a large scale or a small one, never really led to much, beyond some more of the same. There was, he conceded, a good deal of satisfaction in it for a time, but in the long run, the returns started to diminish.

It seemed that things—in some way Commager couldn't quite fathom—should have been arranged differently.

A car passing on the street outside sent a whisper of sound along the edge of his consciousness. With that came the awareness that it had been some time since he'd last heard a car go by and he found himself wondering suddenly what time of night it was.

He glanced at his wristwatch. Three-thirty. A little startled, he tried to compute how long he had been sitting there.

Then it struck him in a surge of panic that he couldn't remember coming to the store at all!

But, of course, his memory told him, you went with Jean to that house...

And Paylar had asked him to sit down and...

What kind of stunt had she pulled on him?

The blackness of terror burst into his consciousness as soon as his thoughts carried him that far—and it wiped out memory. He tried again.

A black explosion. He pushed at it and it retreated a little.

It had been between ten and eleven o'clock. Five hours or so ago. What was the last specific thing he could remember?

HE HAD been sitting in a chair, his eyes closed, a little amused, a little bored. It had been going on for some time. Paylar, a quiet voice off to his left, was asking him a series of odd questions.

PAYLAR: But where are *you*, Mr. Commager?

COMMAGER (tapping his forehead): Right here! Inside my head.

PAYLAR: Could you be more specific about that?

COMMAGER (laughing): I'm somewhere between my ears. Or somewhere back of my eyes.

PAYLAR: How far do you seem to be from the right side of your head? Do you sense the exact distance?

Commager discovered he could sense the exact distance. As a point of awareness, he seemed to be located an inch inside the right side of his skull. Simultaneously, though, he noticed that his left ear was less than an inch and a half away from the same spot—which gave him briefly an odd impression of the general shape of his head!

But he realized then that his attention was shifting around in there, rapidly and imperceptibly. His ears seemed to be now above him, now below and, for a moment, the top of his skull seemed to have moved at least a yard away.

He laughed. "How am I doing?"

Paylar didn't answer. Instead, she asked him to imagine that he was looking at the wall in front of him.

After a while, that wasn't too difficult; Commager seemed to be seeing the wall clearly enough, with a standing lamp in either corner, where Hawkes had placed them. Next, the voice told him to imagine that the same wall now was only a few inches in front of his face—and then that it suddenly had moved six feet behind him. It gave him an odd feeling of having passed straight through the wall in the moment of shifting it.

"Put it twenty feet in front of you again," she said. "And now twenty feet behind you."

Again the sensation of shifting in space, as if he were swinging back and forth, past and through the wall. Commager had become alert and curious now.

On the third swing, he went straight into the blackness...with panic howling around him! After that, everything was blotted out.

HE COULDN'T, Commager discovered, close the gap any farther now. Somewhere near eleven o'clock in the evening, he'd gone into that mental blackout with its peculiarly unpleasant side effects. His next memory might have been twenty minutes ago, when he found himself staring into the miniature underwater forest of the fish tank in his store.

He could phone the Bohart apartment, he thought, and find out what actually had happened. Immediately, then, he became aware of an immense reluctance to carry out that notion and he grimaced irritably. It was no time to worry about what the Boharts might think, but he could imagine Jean's sleepy voice, annoyedly asking who was calling at this hour.

And he'd say, "Well, look, I've lost my memory, I'm afraid. A piece of it anyway—"

He shook his head. After all, they'd gone there to show up the Guides! He'd have to work this out by himself. As if in response to his line of thought, the office telephone, up in the front of the store, began ringing sharply.

The unexpected sound jolted Commager into a set of chills. He sat there stiffly, while the ring was repeated four times; and then, because there was really no reason not to answer it, no matter how improbable it was that someone would be calling the store at this time of night, he got up and started toward the telephone down the long aisle of back-store tanks. Here and there, one of the tanks was illuminated by overhead lights, like the one before which he'd been sitting.

At the corner, where he turned from the aisle into the office, something lay in his path.

He almost stepped on it. He stopped in shock.

It was a slender woman, lying half on her side, half on her face, in a rumpled dress and something like a short white fur jacket. Her loose hair hid her face. The telephone kept on shrilling.

COMMAGER dropped to one knee beside the woman, touched her and knew she was dead, turned her over by the shoulders and felt a stickiness on his hands. There was a slanting cut across her throat, black in the shadows.

"Well," a voice inside Commager's head said with insane calm, "if it isn't Miss MacDonald..." He felt no pity for her at the moment and no real alarm, only a vast amazement.

He realized that the telephone had stopped ringing and clusters of thought burst suddenly and coherently into his awareness again. Somebody apparently thought he was here, at three-thirty in the morning—the same somebody might also suspect that Miss MacDonald was here and even in what condition. And the phone could have been dialed quite deliberately at that moment to bring Commager out of the hypnotized or doped trance, or whatever it was that somebody knew he was trapped in.

In which case, they might be wanting him to discover Ruth MacDonald's body at about this time.

It would be better, he thought, not to get tangled up just now in wondering why anyone should want that to happen; or even whether, just possibly, it had been he himself who had cut Miss MacDonald's brown throat.

What mattered was that, at this instant, somebody was expecting him to react as reasonably as a shocked and stunned man could react in such a situation.

The only really reasonable course of action open to him was to call the police promptly—wherefore, if his curiously calm assumption was correct, he would be primarily expected to do just that. It would be much less reasonable, though still not too unlikely, to carry that ghastly little body far off somewhere and lose it.

Or he could just walk out of here and leave Miss MacDonald on the floor, to be discovered by the store's staff in the morning. That would be a stupid thing to do, but still something that might be expected of a sufficiently dazed and frightened man.

So he wouldn't do any of those things! The hunch was strong in him that the best way to react just now was in a manner unreasonable beyond all calculation.

HE SHOVED Ruth MacDonald's body aside and flicked on his cigarette lighter. On the floor were gummily smeared spots, but she had bled to death somewhere else before she had been dropped here!

Commager's hands and clothes were clean, so it was very improbable that he had carried her in. The sensible thing, he thought, would be to clean up the few stains on the floor before he left, removing any obvious evidence that Miss MacDonald had been in the store at all.

Wherefore, he didn't bother to do it.

Nor did he waste time wondering whether a half dozen tanks in the back part of the store had been lit when he came in here or not. There was a variety of possible reasons why someone might have left a light on over some of them.

He picked up the slender stiffening body on the floor and carried it to the front door.

The door was unlocked and his Hudson was at the curb. He shifted Miss MacDonald to one arm, locked the store door behind him, then placed her in the back seat of the car.

Even Wilshire Boulevard was a lonely street at this hour, but he saw several sets of headlights coming toward him as he got into the car and started it. As far as he could make out, there hadn't been any blood spilled around inside the Hudson, either.

Twelve minutes later, he drove past the corner house he'd visited with Jean Bohart some time before ten in the evening. There was a light on in one of the rooms upstairs, which distinguished Herbert Hawkes's home from any other house in sight. A few blocks away, a dog began to bark.

Dogs might be a problem, he thought.

COMMAGER parked the car a few hundred feet away and sat still for perhaps a minute, listening. The dog stopped barking. Headlights crossed an intersection a few blocks ahead of him.

He got out, lifted Miss MacDonald's body out of the car and walked unhurriedly back to the corner house and over the stepping stones of the dichondra lawn to the side of the house. Here was a trellis, with a gate in it, half open.

Commager eased his burden sideways through the gate. In the half-light of early morning, he set Ruth MacDonald down under a bush—which partly concealed her—in about the same position in which he'd found her. He had a moment of pity to spare for her now.

But there was motion inside the house. Commager looked at the door that opened into this side garden. A vague sequence of motions; somebody walking quietly—but without any suggestion of stealth—was coming closer to the door. Commager stepped quietly up to the wall beside the door and flattened himself against the wall.

A key clicked in the lock. The door swung open. A big shape sauntered out.

Commager's fist was cocked and he struck hard, slanting upward, for the side of the neck and the jaw...

He laid Herbert Hawkes down beside the body of Ruth MacDonald, one big arm draped across her shoulders.

Let the Guides figure that one out, he thought wearily. Not that they wouldn't, of course, but he was going to continue to react unreasonably.

Twenty minutes later, he was in his apartment and sound asleep.

CHAPTER THREE

THE BEDSIDE phone buzzed waspishly. Commager hung for a moment between two levels of awareness. The blazing excitement of the fight was over, but he still hated to relinquish the wild, cold, clear loneliness of the blue—

The thin droning continued to ram at his eardrums. His eyes opened and he sat up, reaching for the telephone as he glanced at the clock beside it. 8:15.

"Alan? I think it worked! Ira had breakfast and drove off to the office, wrapped in deep thought. You were terrific, simply terrific! Just sitting there like a stone wall—"

Commager blinked, trying to catch up with her. Jean Bohart had an athlete's healthy contempt for lie-a-beds and felt no compunction about jolting them out of their torpor. She probably assumed he'd been up and around for the past two hours.

Then his waking memories suddenly flooded back. He sucked in a shocked breath.

"Eh?" She sounded startled.

"I didn't say anything," he managed. "Go ahead—"

He wouldn't, he realized presently, have to ask Jean any leading questions. There was a nervous tension in her that, on occasion, found its outlet in a burst of one-way conversation and this was such an occasion. The Boharts had left the Hawkes home shortly before twelve, Ira apparently depressed by the negative results of the evening. The Reverend Knox had made a phone call somewhat earlier and had been picked up within a few minutes by an elderly woman who, in Jean's phrasing, looked like a French bulldog.

"I think he was glad to get out of there," she added.

COMMAGER didn't comment on that. He himself had stayed on with the others. Ruth MacDonald, in Jean's opinion, was making a pretty definite play for him by that time, while Paylar— "What's her last name, anyway?" —had become withdrawn to the point of rudeness after Commager's spectacular lack of reaction to her psychological games.

"I think she knew just what we were doing by then..." Jean's voice held considerable satisfaction. "So did that Hawkes character. Did you know he's the Herbert Hawkes who owned the Hawkes Chrysler Agency on Figueroa? Well, there's something interesting about that—"

Hawkes had sold out his business about eight months before and it was generally known that his reason had been an imminent nervous breakdown. "What do you make of that, Alan?"

Offhand, Commager admitted, he didn't know what to make of it.

Well, Jean interrupted, she was convinced Hawkes had gone the way Ira would have gone if they hadn't stopped him. "Those Guides have him hypnotized or something," She laughed nervously. "Does it sound as if I'm getting too dramatic about it?"

"No," he said, recalling his last glimpse of Hawkes and his horrid little companion much too vividly. "He doesn't strike me as acting like a man who's been hypnotized, though. Not that I know much about that sort of thing."

Jean was silent, thinking. "Did anything in particular develop between you and MacDonald?" she asked suddenly. There was a strange sharpness in her tone.

Commager felt himself whiten. "No," he said, "I just went home by and by." He tried for a teasing "Are you jealous, little pal?" note. "Were you worrying about it?"

"She's poison, that's all!" Jean said sharply.

AFTER SHE hung up, Commager showered, shaved, dressed and breakfasted, with very little awareness of what he was doing. He was in a frame of mind he didn't entirely understand himself. Under a flow of decidedly unpleasant speculations was a layer of tingling, almost physical elation that—when he stopped to consider it—appeared a less than intelligent response to his present situation. But the realization didn't seem to affect the feeling.

The feeling vanished abruptly when he dumped the clothes he'd been wearing the night before out of the laundry bag into which he had stuffed them, along with the blanket on which he'd laid Ruth MacDonald's body in the car.

He had handled her with some caution and he couldn't discover marks on any of those articles now that seemed likely to incriminate him. But he had no doubt that a more competent investigation could reveal them.

The odd thing was that he still couldn't get himself to worry about such an investigation! He had no logical basis for his belief that unless he himself announced the murder of the secretary of the Parapsychological Group of Long Beach, nobody else was going to take that step. He couldn't even disprove that he hadn't, somewhere along the line last night, dropped into sheer criminal lunacy.

But so far nobody had come pounding at his door to accuse him of murder. And Commager retained the irrationally obstinate conviction that nobody would.

He had an equally strong conviction that he had become the target of the relentless hostility of a group of people, of whose existence he hadn't known until the day before—and that he wouldn't know why until he discovered the reason for his loss of conscious memory in a period during which he had, to Jean Bohart's discerning eyes, showed no noticeable change in behavior.

And, Commager decided finally, he'd better not let the lack of satisfactory conscious evidence for either certainty affect his actions just now.

HE MADE two appointments by telephone and left the apartment an hour after he'd been wakened. A few minutes later, he was at the store, which would open for business at ten o'clock.

Commager unlocked the door and strolled inside. The store's staff had got there at nine and the floors, he noticed, had been thoroughly mopped. Nobody inquired whether he'd been in during the night, so it seemed he had guessed right in leaving the lights on over the big tanks.

He drove into Los Angeles then, to keep his first appointment, at Dr. Henry L. Warbutt's Psychology Center.

Henry was a stout, white-haired, energetic little man with the dark melancholy eyes of one of the great apes. "Thirty minutes for free is all I can spare, even for orphans," he informed Commager. "But you're welcome to that, so come in and sit down, boy! Cup of tea, eh? What do you hear from the Boharts?"

Commager declined the tea, which was likely to be some nasty kind of disguised health-brew, and stated that the Boharts, when last heard from, had been doing fine. It wasn't his first visit to the Center. Both of his parents had been dead before he was twelve and Henry, who was a relative on his father's side, had been his legal guardian until he came of age.

"I want to find out what you know about a new local organization called the Guides," Commager explained.

"They're on the metaphysical side, I'd say, but they seen to be doing some therapy work. They're not listed in the telephone book."

Henry looked slightly disturbed. "If you mean the Guides I'm thinking of, they're not so new. How did you hear about them? Is Ira messing around with that outfit now?"

Commager told him briefly of last night's earlier events, presenting Jean Bohart's version of his own role in them, as if that were the way he recalled it himself.

HENRY became interested at that point. "Do you remember just what those exercises were that the woman put you through?" When Commager had described them, Henry nodded. "They got those gimmicks from another group. I've used them myself now and then. Not on cash clients, of course, just as an experiment. The idea is to divert your attention away from your body-ego, if you know what I mean. No? Well, then—"

He made a steeple of his hands and scowled at his fingertips.

"Metaphysically, it's sometimes used as a method to get you out of your physical body." He waved his hands vaguely around. "Off you go into the astral plane or something!" He grinned. "Understand now?"

"More or less," Commager said doubtfully. "Did you ever see it happen?"

"Eh? Oh, no... With me, they usually just go to sleep. Or else they get bored and won't react at all, about like you did. There's no therapeutic value in it that I know of. But probably no harm, either."

"Would you say whether there's any harm in the Guides?"

"Well," said Henry thoughtfully, "they're certainly one of the more interesting groups of our local psychological fauna. Personally, I wouldn't go out of my way to antagonize them.

Of course, Ira's such a damn fool, you probably had to do something pretty obvious to discourage him. Fifteen or twenty years ago, the Guides were working principally with drugs, as far as I could make out at the time. I don't know whether this is the same organization or not, but just lately...the last year or so...I've been hearing gossip about them again."

"What kind of gossip?"

"WELL, YOU know a good many of the people who come into this Center for therapy are interested in metaphysics in one way or another," Henry explained. "Some of them have been telling me lately that the Guides are the latest thing in a True Group. And a True Group, in their language, means chiefly that the people in it have some honest-to-goodness supernatural abilities and powers..."

He grimaced unhappily. "Another characteristic is that nobody else knows exactly who belongs to a True Group. In that way, your acquaintances seem to be living up to the legend."

Commager said he'd been under the impression that the Guides dealt in parapsychology.

Henry nodded. "Well, they'd use that, too, of course. Depending on the class of client—" He hesitated briefly. "By and large I'd say the Guides were a very good outfit for fairly normal citizens like you and the Boharts to stay away from..."

He'd also heard of the Reverend Wilson Knox and of the Temple of Antique Christianity, though not favorably.

"Knox has a crummy little sect back in one of the Hollywood canyons. They go in for Greek paganism. Strictly a screwball group." He didn't know anything of the Parapsychological Group of Long Beach. "You can't keep up with all of them."

CHAPTER FOUR

JULIUS SAVAGE was a lanky, sun-browned hypnotist who'd sometimes gone spear fishing with Commager. On one such occasion (the last, if Julius had anything to say about it) Commager had been obliged to haul him half-drowned out of a kelp bed and thump him back into consciousness. Which made him the right man right now.

He clasped his hands behind his head, rocked himself back from his desk and looked first interested and then highly dubious, while Commager went on talking.

"You're about as lousy a hypnotic subject as I am myself, Alan!" Julius protested finally. "I tried to put you under twice, remember? Anyway, how about sending you to my tame M.D. for a check-up first? Amnesia isn't anything to— No?" He considered. "Well, how long ago did this happen?"

The fact that it had happened only the night before reassured him somewhat. So presently Commager was sitting in an armchair being informed that his eyelids were getting heavier and heavier.

An hour later, Julius said discouragedly, "This isn't getting us anywhere and I've got another appointment at two o'clock. How bad do you want that information, Alan?"

"It's a matter of life and death…"

"Oh, hell!" said Julius. He went out of the room and came back with a small bottle, partly filled with a slightly oily, aromatic liquid. "I don't use this often, but… By the way, with the possible exception of last night, did anyone else ever try to hypnotize you?"

"Ira Bohart did, the first time I met him," Commager recalled. "It was at a party. No results."

"We'll make it two spoonfuls," Julius decided.

TEN MINUTES later, Commager got into the blackness. The next time he consciously opened his eyes, it was past three in the afternoon. Julius, looking pale and exhausted, stood at the desk watching him. He'd loosened his tie and hung his jacket over the back of a chair. His hair was disheveled.

"Brother!" he remarked. "Well...we got something, Alan. I'll play parts of it back to you." He jerked his head at a gently burbling percolator on a mantel. "Cup of coffee there for you. Better have some."

Commager sipped black coffee, yawned, and took note of the time. Too much of the day already was past, he thought uneasily; he wondered what the Guides had been doing meanwhile. "What happened to your appointments?"

"Canceled them," Julius said, fiddling with the tape recorder. "They'll keep." He glanced around at Commager. "Here's the first thing we got. Chronologically, it seems to fit in at the end of the period you can't remember. Symbolism, but I'm curious. We'll try it first."

Commager listened. After a while, there were pricklings of memory. When Julius stopped the recorder, he remarked, "I had a dream this morning that seems to tie in with that."

"Ah?" Julius looked professionally cautious. "Well, let's hear about it."

Commager hesitated. The dream seemed irrelevant and rather childish, like a fairy tale. He'd been flying around in a great open space, he began at last. And he'd been wondering why nobody else was up there with him, but he hadn't felt particularly concerned about it. Then a hawk came swooping at him, trying to knock him out of the air.

THE TIES OF EARTH

There was a long leash attached to the hawk's leg and Commager noticed that, far down below, a number of people were holding the leash and watching the battle. "That explained why there wasn't anyone else around, you see. When anyone tried it, they simply sent a hawk up after him."

"Hm!" said Julius. "Recognize the people?"

"No—" Commager checked himself and laughed. "Of course, it just struck me! Hawkes was the name of one of the people I met last night! That explains the dream!"

Julius nodded doubtfully. "Possibly. How did it continue?"

AS COMMAGER recalled it, there hadn't been much more to it. He couldn't damage the hawk and the hawk couldn't bring him down; finally it disappeared. Then he'd been up there alone—and then he'd been wakened by the telephone.

Julius tapped the desk with the eraser end of a pencil, looking thoughtful. "Well..." he sighed. He turned to the recorder. "Let's try another part of this now, Alan. The central part. Incidentally, we didn't get into what you were actually doing last night. These are your subjective impressions and they aren't necessarily an immediately recognizable reflection of real events, past or present. You understand that?"

Commager said he did. But he felt a stab of sharp apprehension. He was reasonably certain that whatever Julius heard or guessed in his office remained a private matter. But his own line of action had been based on the solid personal conviction that, whatever had happened last night, it hadn't been he who had killed Ruth MacDonald.

In view of the hypnotist's careful and almost formal phrasing, Commager was, for a few moments at least, not quite so sure about that.

They were a bad few moments…

Then the recorder was turning again.

"WHAT DO you make of it?" Julius asked. "It will help me formulate my own opinion."

Commager shrugged. He still felt shaken, after the intermittent waves of grief, rage and remorse that had pounded through him while a section of the tape rewound itself again—with a vividness and immediacy that dazed him, but still seemed rather unaccountable. After all, that had been over and done with almost four years ago!

"It's fairly obvious to me," he said reluctantly. At least his voice sounded steady enough. "A few months before my wife died, I'd begun to get interested in the ESP experiments she was playing around with. You remember Lona was almost as bad that way as Ira Bohart."

He managed a brief, careful grin. "It annoyed me at first, but, of course, I didn't let her know. I thought she'd drop it soon enough. When she didn't, I decided I'd experiment on the quiet by myself. Actually, I was after information I could use to convince Lona she was wasting her time with that sort of thing—and then she'd have more time to spare for the kind of fun and games I was interested in."

Julius smiled faintly and nodded.

"I STARTED making lists of coincidences," Commager explained. "Occasions when I'd tell myself Lona would be home at six, say, and she'd actually show up about that time. Or I'd decide what dress she'd select to wear the next morning—"

"Predictions, generally?" Julius drew a precise little circle on the desk blotter with his pencil and studied it critically.

"Yes. Or I'd put the idea into her head that she wanted to talk about some particular thing with me—and sometimes she would." Commager smiled. "I was also, you see, keeping a list of the times these little experiments didn't work out, and they often didn't…at first. So that, when I finally told Lona about it, it would be obvious that the coincidences had been just that."

He hesitated. "I still think they were just that. But one day, it struck me I'd accumulated too many coincidences lately. It shook me."

"Did it stop your experimentation?" Julius remained intent on the circle he'd drawn.

"A few days later, it did," Commager said. He discovered suddenly that he was sweating. "Lona phoned me that afternoon that she was driving down to the beach to pick me up. After she hung up, I had a sudden positive feeling that if she drove her car that afternoon, she'd get killed! I almost called her back. But I decided I wasn't going to let myself turn into another Ira Bohart. As of then, I was quitting all this ESP business and so was Lona. When she got there, I'd tell her—"

The sweat was running down his face now. "Well, you know that part of it. Lona had a heart attack while driving, the doctors thought, and crashed and got killed." He paused again, because his voice had begun to shake. "I don't know why that got on there…" He nodded at the recorder. "…except that last night was the first time since that horrible event four years ago that I felt…even for a minute…that something might be going on that couldn't be explained in a perfectly normal way."

"THAT," inquired Julius, "was while you were going through that peculiar set of exercises you were describing, wasn't it? Alan, how long ago has it been, exactly, since your wife died?"

"Not quite four years." Commager drove back a surge of impatience. "I suppose I've felt guilty enough about it ever since! But right now, Julius, I'm interested in finding out why I lost a few hours of memory last night and how to restore them. Are we getting any closer to that?"

"I think we are. Can you be at this office at 10 A.M. two days from tomorrow? That's Thursday morning..."

"Why then?"

Julius shrugged. "Because that's the earliest appointment I could make for you with Dr. Ciardi. I phoned him just before you woke up. He's a friend of mine and an excellent psychiatrist, Alan. We do a lot of work together."

Commager said in angry amazement, "Damn you, Julius! I told you I didn't want anyone else to know about this!"

"I know," Julius admitted unhappily. "We've been fairly good friends for about eight years now, haven't we? We've been in and out of each other's homes and met each other's acquaintances, right?"

Commager's fingertips drummed on his right knee. He was still furious. "So what?"

"So *hell*, Alan! What you were telling me just now never happened! Your wife wasn't killed in an auto accident four years ago because, four years ago, you didn't have a wife! To the best of my knowledge, you've never been married!"

CHAPTER FIVE

COMMAGER had a rather early dinner at Tilford's. A mirror lined the entire wall on the opposite side of the room. Now and then he glanced at his reflection. For a sort of lunatic, he thought, the big, sun-tanned man sitting there looked remarkably calm and healthy.

He was still amazed, above all, at the apparent instantaneousness with which he had realized what Julius had blurted out was true! He could picture Lona in a hundred different ways, very vividly, but he couldn't actually recall having ever mentioned her to anybody else! And he couldn't now remember a single time when he and she and any other person had been together.

It was almost as if the entire episode of Lona had been a story somebody had told him, illustrated out of his own imaginings. And now, in a few hours, the story was beginning to fade out. Specific scenes had dropped almost beyond the reach of memory. The image of Lona herself started to blur.

HIS immediate reaction had been an odd mixture of shocked self-disgust and profound relief, threaded with the feeling that actually he'd always known, without being consciously aware of it, that there wasn't any real Lona.

Even the emotions he'd felt while listening to the tape recorder were a part of the fabrication; almost at the instant of realization, they began to break away from him. Like the sudden shattering of a hard shell of alien matter that he'd been dragging around—rather like a hermit crab—under the pretense that it was a natural part of himself. The self-disgust became even more pronounced at that comparison.

But whatever his original motives had been for imposing that monstrous construction upon his mind, Commager couldn't see any further connection between it and the events of the past night.

Apparently he had thrust himself into a period of amnesia to avoid the full impact of an artificial set of emotions. In that period, there had been a very real and very unpleasant occurrence—a murder.

His main reason now for remaining convinced that he hadn't been the murderer was that the evening papers carried no indication that the body of Ruth MacDonald had been found.

Which certainly indicated guilt on the part of those who must have found her.

He could afford to wait until Thursday, Commager decided, to go digging after the causes of his delusion under Dr. Ciardi's guidance. But he probably couldn't afford to wait at all to find out what the Guides—he still had to assume it was the Guides—were preparing for him next.

And perhaps the best way to find out would be, quite simply, to ask.

HE FINISHED his dinner, walked up the street to a telephone booth and dialed the number of Herbert Hawkes's home. A man's voice informed him presently that it was the Hawkes residence, Lex Barthold speaking.

That, Commager recalled, was the name of the blond young man who had been an untalkative member of the party last night. He gave his own name and said he was trying to contact Miss Paylar—a piece of information that produced a silence of several seconds at the other end. But when Barthold spoke again, he sounded unshaken.

"Paylar isn't in at the moment. Shall I take your message, Mr. Commager?"

Commager said no, he'd try again, and hung up. Now that, he reflected, walking back to his car, seemed to be an interesting sort of household...

For the first time since leaving Julius's office, he wasn't too displeased with himself. If he saw Paylar alone, he might, as far as appearances went, be taking an interest in the well-being of Ira Bohart or, reasonably enough, in Paylar herself.

And things could start developing from that point.

Of course, she might avoid letting him see her alone. In any case, his call would give them something new to consider.

He drove to the beach and turned south toward San Diego. A half-hour later, he parked before the cabin where, among bulkier items of fishing gear, he kept a 45-caliber revolver. He put that in the glove compartment of the car and started back to town.

THE TELEPHONE rang a few minutes after he reached his apartment.

"I've called you twice in the last hour," Paylar said. "I understand you want to speak to me."

"I do," said Commager. "Do you happen to have the evening free?"

She laughed. "I've arranged to have it free. You can meet me at your aquarium store, Mr. Commager."

"Eh?" he said stupidly.

"At your store." Her voice still sounded amused. "You see, I may have a business proposition for you."

Then the line went dead.

Commager swore and hung up. When he turned into Wilshire Boulevard not very many minutes later, he saw a long gray car, vague under the streetlights, move away from the curb a hundred feet or so beyond his store and drive off. There was no sign of Paylar.

He parked and followed the car thoughtfully with his eyes. Then he got out. The store was locked, the interior dark. But in back of the office, behind the partition, was a shimmering of light.

He thought of the gun in his car. There had been one murder. It seemed a little early for another one.

He unlocked the door and locked it again behind him. This time, there were no bodies lying around the aisles. But at the back of the store, standing before a lighted fish tank and looking into it, Paylar was waiting for him.

HE DIDN'T ask her how she got in. It seemed a theatrical gesture, a boasting indication that his affairs could be easily invaded from without. Aside from that, the darkened store undoubtedly was a nice place for an ambush. Commager wondered briefly why he didn't feel more concerned about that and realized then that he was enormously angry. An ambush might have been a relief.

"Did you find out much about us today?" Paylar asked.

"Not enough," he admitted. "Perhaps you can tell me more."

"That's why I'm here."

Commager looked at her skeptically. She was wearing a black sweater and slacks that appeared wine-colored in the inadequate light from the big tank. A small, finely shaped body and a small, vivid face. The mouth smiled soberly; black eyes gleamed like an animal's as she turned her head toward him.

"We're an organization," she said, "that operates against the development of parapsychological abilities in human beings…"

Oddly enough, it made sense and he found himself believing her. Then he laughed. "Do you object to my winning a crap game?"

Paylar said seriously, "We don't object to that. But you're not stopping there, Mr. Commager."

Again there was an instant of inner agreement; an elation and anxiety. Commager hesitated, startled by his reaction. He said, "I'm not aware of any ambition along that line."

She shook her head. "I don't think you're being quite truthful. But it doesn't really matter how aware you are of it just now. The last twenty-four hours have indicated clearly that you can't be checked by any ordinary methods." She frowned. "The possibility had been foreseen—and so we hit you with everything that was immediately available, Mr. Commager. I was sure it was enough."

Commager felt a little bewildered. "Enough for what?"

"Why, almost anybody else would have done something sensible—and then refused to ever budge out of the everyday world again, even in his thoughts. Instead, you turned around and started to smoke us out—which, incidentally, saved you for the moment from an even more unnerving experience..."

COMMAGER stared at her, appalled. That final comment had no present meaning for him, but she obviously was speaking about a murder of which she—at the very least—had known at the time. She considered it mildly amusing that it had backfired on them!

He said harshly, "I'd enjoy breaking your neck. But I suspect that you're a little crazy."

She shrugged, smiling. "The trouble is that you're not going to go on thinking that, Mr. Commager. If you did, we could safely disregard you."

He looked down at his hands. "So what are you going to do?"

"There are others who say you can be stopped. It's certain you won't like their methods, though I'm not entirely sure they will be effective. I came here tonight to offer you an alternative."

"Go ahead and offer it."

"You can join us," she said.

Commager gave a short laugh of sheer astonishment. "Now why should I want to do that?"

"In the end," Paylar said soberly, "you may have very little choice. But there's another reason. You've been trying, all your life, to bring your abilities into your consciousness and under your control."

He shook his head. "If you mean wild talents, I haven't done anything of the sort."

"Unfortunately," she said, "you won't remain unaware of that trend in yourself very much longer. And, if you cooperate with us, we can and will help you to do just that. But we can't let you continue by yourself, without safeguards. You're too likely to be successful, you see. Those wild talents can become extremely wild!"

"You know," he said, almost good-humoredly, "I think you really believe what you say. But as far as I'm concerned, you're a group of criminal lunatics without any more secret ability than I have myself..."

"That," Paylar replied undisturbed, "is precisely what we're afraid of. For the time being, though, we can use our abilities in ways that you cannot. What happened while you were doing those exercises last night, Mr. Commager?"

He looked at her and then away. "I got rather bored."

PAYLAR laughed. "You're lying. Exercises of that kind provide very convincing illusions, and very little else, for people who are hungry for illusion. But since you have an ability, it took no more than a word to bring it into action! That was when we knew you had to be stopped. However, I'm afraid you're still turning down my offer."

"You read my mind that time, lady. I'd turn you over to the police, too, if I thought it would do any good."

"It wouldn't," she assured him. Her head tilted a moment, with soft grace, into an attitude of listening. "I think my car is coming back for me. I'll leave that offer open, Mr. Commager—in case you survive long enough now to except it…"

He grinned. "You shouldn't frighten me like that."

"I've frightened you a little, but not nearly enough. But there is more than one way to shake a man to his senses—or out of them—so perhaps we can still change your mind. Would you let me out the front door now?"

Lights slid over the ceiling above her as she spoke, and the long gray car, its engine throbbing, stood at the curb when they came out. Paylar turned at the car door.

"You know where I'm staying," she said, looking up at him, "if you want to find me."

Commager nodded.

She smiled and then the door opened for her and light briefly filled the interior of the car.

Seconds later, he stood staring after it as it fled down the street. She'd been right about there being more than one way of shaking a man out of his senses.

The driver of the car—the very much alive driver—had been Ruth MacDonald!

UNDER WHAT wasn't quite a full Moon tonight, the Bay would have looked artificial if it hadn't been so huge. A savage, wild place, incongruous in this area with the slow thump and swirl and thunder of the tide.

A mile to the south was a cluster of cottages down near the water's edge. Commager's cabin was as close as anything could have been built to the flank of the big northern drop-off. He could look down at the sharp turn of the highway below him or out at the Bay. Nobody yet had tried to build on the rocky rises of ground behind him.

Without ordinary distractions, it was a good place for a few hours of painstaking reorientation. He wasn't exactly frightened, Commager told himself. But when he had recognized Ruth MacDonald, a wave of unreason inside him had seemed to rise to meet and merge with the greater wave of unreason rolling in from a shadow-world without. For that moment, the rules of reality had flickered out of existence.

An instant later, he'd had them solidly re-established. He was now simply a man who knew something had happened that he couldn't begin to explain rationally. It was a much more acceptable situation, since it included the obvious explanation of irrationality.

On Thursday morning, he could tell Dr. Ciardi, "Look, Doc, I'm having hallucinations. The last one was a honey. I thought I was carrying a dead woman all over town! What do we do about it?"

And they'd do whatever was done in such circumstances and it would be a sane, normal, active life for Alan Commager forever after—with a woman more or less like Jean Bohart to live it with, which would keep out the shadowy Lonas. With everything, in fact, that didn't fit into that kind of life, that belonged to the shadow-worlds, as completely obliterated and forgotten as they could become.

Commager wondered what made that picture look so unsatisfactory.

IT STRUCK him suddenly that, according to Paylar, this was exactly how the Guides had expected him to react as soon as her little games had steered him into a bout of amnesia and hallucinations. They'd wanted, she'd said, in approximately those words, to put him in a frame of mind that would make him refuse to ever budge out of the safe, everyday world again, even in his thoughts.

Commager grimaced. But they'd become convinced then that he wasn't going to do it...

He might do it all the same, he thought. But the reason it couldn't be a completely satisfactory solution was growing clear. One couldn't discount the probability that there was a little more to the shadow-worlds than lunacy and shadow. Perhaps only a very little more and perhaps not. But if he avoided looking at what was there, he would never find out.

And then he realized that he wasn't going to avoid looking at it, hadn't really been seriously considering it. He swore at himself, because avoidance did seem still the simple and rational solution, providing one could be satisfied with it.

He couldn't be satisfied with it and that was that. He could see now that if an organization such as Paylar had described the Guides to be existed, and if it were composed, at least in part, of people who really had developed an understanding and working knowledge of the possibilities of PSI, it would be in a uniquely favorable position to control and check the development of similar abilities in others.

Its connections and its influence would be primarily with the psychological fringe groups here and with their analogs elsewhere; and the people who were drawn to such groups would be those who were dissatisfied with or incompetent in normal lines of activity, and had become abnormally interested in compensating for their lack of other achievement by investigating the shadowy, vague, ego-bolstering promise of PSI.

And people frightened by the threat of total war, driven into a search for psychic refuge by the prospect of physical destruction.

In either case, because they were uncertain, less than normally capable people, they could be controlled without too much difficulty—and carefully diverted then, in groups or as individuals, from the thing they were seeking and might stumble upon!

The exercises she'd demonstrated to him, Paylar had said, were designed primarily to provide convincing illusions for those who were hungry for illusion.

SHE AND her associates, Commager realized, might feel it was necessary. They might know just enough to be afraid of what such knowledge could lead to. If it were possible to encourage a pair of dice to bounce and spin in just the right pattern to win for you, it might, for example, also be possible to send a few buildings bouncing and spinning through a city! Of course, nobody ever seemed to have done it, but that might be due precisely to the existence of some controlling agency, such as the Guides claimed to be.

For a while, Commager regarded the possibility of accepting Paylar's invitation to join her group—and, a few seconds later, he knew he wasn't going to do that either.

However determined he might be to proceed with a painstaking and thorough investigation of this field of possibilities now, there was still a feeling of something completely preposterous about the entire business.

He could accept the fact that he had been shaken up mentally to the point where he might qualify without too much difficulty for the nearest insane asylum. But he wasn't ready to admit to anybody just yet that he, a grown man, was taking the matter of PSI very seriously.

It was something you could try out for yourself, just as an experiment, behind locked doors and with the windows shaded.

So Commager locked the front door to his cabin and tried it out.

CHAPTER SIX

THE TELEGRAM that had been shoved under his apartment door during the night gave a Hollywood telephone number and urgently requested him to call it. It was signed by Elaine Lovelock. So far as Commager could remember, Elaine was no one he knew. When he dialed the number, nobody answered.

He'd try to reach her again before he left for the store, he decided. It was eight-thirty now; he'd just got in from the Bay. The chances were somebody's deluxe fifty-gallon tropical fish tank had started to leak on the living room carpet, and it hadn't occurred to them immediately that this was what pails and pots were for.

He sat down to write a few notes on last night's experiment. Nothing very striking had happened; he suspected he'd simply fallen asleep after the first forty minutes or so. But if he kept notes, something like a recognizable pattern might develop.

Item: The "Lona complex" hadn't bothered him much. It was beginning to feel like something that had happened to somebody else a long time ago. So perhaps the emotions connected with it hadn't been triggered by Paylar's exercises, as Julius seemed to assume. Or else, since he no longer believed in it, it was on its way out as a complex—he hoped.

Item: With his eyes closed, he could imagine very easily that he was looking through the wall of the room into another section of the cabin; also that he had moved there in person, as a form of awareness. In fact, he had roamed happily all around the Bay area for about ten minutes. For the present, that proved only that he had a much more vivid imagination than he'd thought—though whoever created Lona could be assumed to have considerable hidden talent along that line!

Item: When he'd tried to "read" specific pages of a closed book lying on a table near him, he had failed completely.

Item: He had run suddenly—he might have been asleep by then—into successive waves of unexplained panic, which brought him upright in his chair with his pulses hammering wildly.

Item: The panic had faded out of reach the instant he began to investigate it and he hadn't been able to recall it.

Item: Either shortly before or after that event, he'd had for a while the sensation of being the target of stealthy and malevolent observation. He had made an attempt to "locate" the observer and gained the impression that the other one unhurriedly withdrew.

Item: Briefly, he'd had a feeling of floating up near the ceiling of the room, watching his own body sitting in the armchair with its eyes closed. This had rocked him hard enough to awaken him again and he had concluded the experiments.

Item: After waking up, he hadn't found or imagined he'd found Ruth MacDonald or anybody else lying around the cabin, murdered or otherwise. He'd checked.

And that about summed it up, Commager decided. Not very positive results, but he was determined to continue the experiments.

He suspected Julius would feel very dubious about all this; but Julius wasn't going to be informed.

He himself was in a remarkably cheerful mood this morning.

MRS. LOVELOCK had a magnificent, musical voice, rather deep for a woman.

"I'm so glad you called again, Mr. Commager," she said. "I was away on an unavoidable errand. Dr. Knox needs to see you immediately. How soon can you be here?"

"Dr. Knox?" Commager repeated. "Do you mean the Reverend Wilson Knox?"

"That is correct. Do you have the address of our Temple?"

Commager said he didn't. There was no immediate reason to add that he hadn't the slightest intention of going there, either. "What did he want to see me about?"

Mrs. Lovelock hesitated. "I couldn't explain it satisfactorily by telephone, Mr. Commager." A trace of anxiety came into her voice. "But it's quite urgent..."

Commager said he was sorry; he had a very full business day ahead of him—which was true—so, unless he could get some indication of what this was all about—

The melodious voice told him quaveringly, "Dr. Knox had a serious heart attack last night. He needs your help..."

Commager scowled. She sounded as off-beat as the rest of them and he had an urgent impulse to hang up.

He said instead, "I don't quite see how I could be of much help under those circumstances. I'm not a doctor, you know."

"I do know that, Mr. Commager," Mrs. Lovelock replied. "I also know that you haven't been acquainted with Dr. Knox for more than a few days. But I assure you that you may be saving a human life by coming out here immediately. And that is all I can tell you now—"

She stopped short, sounding as if she were about to burst into tears.

What she said didn't make sense. Also Commager hadn't liked the Reverend Knox, quite aside from the company he kept. But he could, he supposed resignedly, afford to waste a few more hours now.

THE TIES OF EARTH

"What was that address?" he asked, trying not to sound too ungracious about it.

ON THE way over, he had time to wonder whether this mightn't be part of some new little game the Guides wanted to play with him. He was inclined to discount Paylar's threats—psychologically he suspected they'd already tried everything they could do to him—and they didn't look like people who would resort readily to physical violence, though Hawkes could be an exception there.

When Commager came in sight of the Temple of Antique Christianity, physical violence suddenly looked a little more likely. He stopped a moment to consider the place.

It was in a back canyon beyond Laurel; the last quarter—mile had been a private road. A tall iron gate blocked the road at this point, opening into a walled court with a small building to the right. A sign over a door in the building indicated that this was the office.

Some distance back, looming over the walls of the court and a few intervening trees, was another structure, an old white building in the Spanish style, the size of a small hotel.

It looked like the right kind of setting for the kind of screwball cult Henry Warbutt had described. Depending on who was around, it also looked like a rather good place for murder or mayhem.

Should he just stroll in carelessly like a big, brave, athletic man? Or should he be a dirty coward and get his revolver out of the glove compartment? It was bound to make an unsightly bulge in any of his jacket pockets.

He decided to be a dirty coward.

THE GATE was locked, but the lock clicked open a few seconds after Commager pushed a buzzer button beside it.

The only visible way into the area was through the office door, so he went inside.

A pallid young man and a dark, intense-looking young woman sat at desks across the room from the door. The young man told Commager he was expected and went to a side door of the office with him, from where he pointed to an entrance into the big building, on the other end of what he called the grove.

"Mrs. Lovelock is waiting for you there," he said and went back to his desk.

The grove had the reflective and well-preserved air of a section of an exclusive cemetery, with just enough trees growing around to justify its name. There was a large, square lawn in the center, and a large, chaste bronze statue stood at each corner of the lawn, gazing upon it.

Back among trees to the left was a flat, raised platform, apparently faced with gray and black marble, but otherwise featureless. Commager had just gone past this when he realized that somebody had been watching him from the top of the platform as he passed.

That, at any rate, was the feeling he got. He hadn't actually seen anyone, and when he looked back, there was nobody there. But the feeling not only had been a definite and certain one—it resumed the instant he started walking on again. This time, he didn't look back.

Before he'd gone a dozen more steps, he knew, too, just when he'd experienced that exact sensation before. It was the previous night, while he was doing his parapsychological experiments at the Bay and had suddenly felt that he was under secret and unfriendly scrutiny.

He laughed at himself, but the impression remained a remarkably vivid one. And before he reached the entrance to the main building that the young man in the office had indicated to him, he had time for the thought that playing with the imagination, as he was doing, might leave one eventually on very shaky ground.

Then he was there, looking into a long hallway, and Mrs. Lovelock's fine, deep voice greeted him before he caught sight of her.

"I'm so glad you could come, Mr. Commager," she said.

SHE WAS standing in the door of a room that opened on the hall to the left, and Commager was a trifle startled by her appearance. He had expected a large handsome woman of about thirty, to match the voice. But Mrs. Lovelock was not only huge; she was shockingly ugly and probably almost twice the age he'd estimated. She wore a white uniform, so Commager asked whether she was Wilson Knox's nurse.

"I've been a registered nurse for nearly forty years, Mr. Commager," the beautiful voice told him. "At present, I'm attending Dr. Knox. Would you come in here, please?"

He followed her into the room and she closed the door behind them. Her big, gray face, Commager decided, looked both worried and very angry.

"The reason I wasn't more open with you over the telephone," she told him, "was that I was certain you wouldn't have taken the trouble to drive out here if I had been. And I couldn't have blamed you! Won't you sit down, please?"

Commager took a chair. "I'm afraid I don't understand."

Mrs. Lovelock nodded. "I shall give you the facts. Dr. Knox had a very severe heart attack at around two o'clock this morning. I have been a member of his congregation for twenty-four years, and I arrived with a doctor shortly afterward. Dr. Knox is resting comfortably now, but he is very anxious to see you. I must let him tell you why, Mr. Commager. But I should like to prepare you for what you will hear—"

MRS. LOVELOCK stared gloomily at the carpet for a moment and then her face twisted briefly into a grimace of pure rage.

"Wilson—Dr. Knox—is a harmless old fool!" she told Commager savagely. "This Antique Christianity he worked out never hurt anybody. They prayed to Pan and they had their dances and chants. And there was the Oracle and he read out of the Book of Pan..."

"I don't know anything about Dr. Knox's activities," Commager said, not too politely.

She had thick, reddened, capable hands and they were locked together now on her lap, the fingers twisting slowly against one another, as if she were trying to break something between them.

"I was the Oracle, you see," she explained. "I knew it was foolish, but I'd sit up there on the dais in the smoke, with a veil over my head, and I'd say whatever I happened to think of. But this year, Wilson brought in that Ruth MacDonald— I believe you already know her?"

"I've met the lady," Commager admitted. "I wouldn't say I know her."

"She became the Oracle! And then she began to change everything. I told Wilson he was quite right to resist that. There are things, Mr. Commager, that a good Christian simply must not do..."

Which, Commager felt, was a remarkable statement, under the circumstances. Mrs. Lovelock came ponderously to her feet.

"Dr. Knox will tell you what remains to be told," she added rather primly. "And, of course, you cannot stay too long. Will you follow me now, please?"

THE REVEREND didn't look as if he were in too bad a condition, Commager thought when he saw him first. He was lying in a hospital bed that had been raised high enough to let him gaze down at the grove out of the window of his second-story room.

After he'd talked a few moments, Commager felt the man was delirious and he thought briefly of calling back Mrs. Lovelock or the other nurse—who had been with Wilson Knox when they came in. But those two undoubtedly had been able to judge for themselves whether they should remain with the Reverend or not.

"Why should they want to kill you?" Commager asked. Knox had been speaking of the Guides and then had started to weep; now he blew his nose on a piece of tissue and made a groping motion for Commager's hand, which Commager withdrew.

"It was merely a matter of business as far as I was concerned, Mr. Commager. I certainly had no intention of blocking any activities of the Guides. In fact, I should prefer not to know about them. But when Miss MacDonald, who was employed by the Temple, upset our members, I protested to her, sir! Isn't that understandable?"

"Entirely," Commager agreed carefully. "What did Miss MacDonald do to upset them?"

"She predicted two of the congregation would die before the end of the year," Wilson Knox said shakily. "It caused a great deal of alarm. Many of our wealthier clients withdrew from the Temple at once. It is a considerable financial loss!"

The Reverend appeared rational enough on that point. Commager inquired, "Is Miss MacDonald one of the Guides, Dr. Knox?"

"It's not for me to say." Knox gave him a suddenly wary look. "When she spoke to me by telephone last night, I asked whether I had offended anyone. I was, of course, greatly distressed!" His expression changed back to one of obvious and profound self-pity. "But she repeated only that it had become necessary for me to die this week and hung up."

IT SEEMED an odd way at that for the Temple's new Oracle to have phrased her prediction, Commager thought. He regarded Dr. Knox without much sympathy. "So now you want me to simply tell her not to hurt you, eh?"

"It would be better, Mr. Commager," Knox suggested, "if you addressed yourself directly to the young woman called Paylar!" He reached for his visitor's hand again. "I place myself under your protection, sir. I know you won't refuse me."

Which was almost precisely what he had said as soon as the nurses left the room, and the reason Commager had believed the patient was in a state of delirium. Now it seemed more probable that he was merely badly mistaken.

Commager decided not to ask why it would be better to speak to Paylar. At any direct question concerning the Guides, the Reverend became evasive. He said instead, "What made you decide I could protect you, Dr. Knox?"

Knox looked downright crafty. "I have made no inquiries about you, sir, and I do not intend to. I am a simple man whose life has been devoted to providing a measure of beauty and solace for his fellow human beings. In a modest way, of course. I have never pried into the Greater Mysteries!"

He seemed to expect approval for that, so Commager nodded gravely.

"I speak only of what I saw," Wilson Knox continued. "On Sunday night, I saw them attempt to bring you directly under their sway. Forgive me for saying, sir, that they do not do this with an ordinary person! I also saw them fail and I knew they were frightened. Nevertheless, you were not destroyed."

He tapped Commager's hand significantly. "That, sir, was enough for me. I do not attempt to pry—I have merely placed myself under your protection!"

CHAPTER SEVEN

A MAN with Secret Powers, a man who could tell the Guides to go jump in the Pacific, might take a passing interest in the gimmicks of an organization like the Temple of Antique Christianity. So on his way out through the grove, Commager had turned aside to get a closer look at the dais.

He assumed, at least, that the gray and black marble platform was what Mrs. Lovelock had referred to as the seat of the Oracle, since nothing else around seemed suitable for the purpose.

Standing before it, he pictured her sitting up there in the night, veiled, a vast, featureless bulk, announcing whatever came into her mind in that stunning voice, and he could see that Wilson Knox's congregation might well have listened in pop-eyed fascination. Ruth MacDonald couldn't have been nearly as impressive. Perhaps that was why she had started passing out death sentences.

Down on Sunset, he parked his car at the curb and remained in it, watching the traffic, while he tried to digest the information he had received—if you could call it information.

Wilson Knox and Mrs. Lovelock appeared to be people who had fabricated so much fantastic garbage for the clients of the Temple that they had no judgment left to resist the fabrications of others.

Commager's parting from Mrs. Lovelock had given him the impression that the huge woman also was sullenly afraid, though she hid it much better than the Reverend had. It could be simply that she felt her own position in the Temple would be lost if Knox died; but he thought that in her case, too, it was a more personal fear, of the Guides, or even of himself.

And he'd practically promised both of them to put in a word with Paylar to protect that revolting little man!

HOWEVER, the Reverend's heart attack, at least, probably had been a real enough thing.   And if Ruth MacDonald actually had telephoned a prediction of death to him earlier in the night, there was some cause for intervention.   The practice of frightening people into their graves was something that anyone could reasonably insist should be stopped!

And that, of course, brought up the question of how he expected to stop it.

And the question, once more, of just what that odd group of people—who indicated they were the Guides or associated with them—was after.

Ruth MacDonald's activities concerning the Temple of Antique Christianity hardly seemed to lie on the lofty, idealistic level he'd been almost willing to ascribe to them in theory, even if he disliked their methods.   She was a brassy, modern young witch, Commager thought, using the old witchcraft tools of fear and suggestion out of equally old motives of material gain and prestige.

But one couldn't account for Hawkes as simply as that, because Hawkes had had money and prestige.

Commager knew least of all about Paylar, except for the young man called Lex Barthold, whose connection with the others wasn't clear.   The impression of Paylar was still mainly that she had a physical personality that would be hard to match if you liked them slender, dark and mysterious, and with a self-assurance that wasn't aggressive like Ruth MacDonald's, but that might be a great more difficult to crack. Among the three he'd had to deal with, she seemed to be the leader, though that wasn't necessarily true.

He found himself walking slowly down the street toward a phone booth.

Let's make a game of it, he thought. Assume that what Paylar had said and what the Reverend had suspected was true—at least in the Guides's own opinion—that he had turned out to be exceptionally tough material for their psychological gimmicks. That he had, in fact, abilities he didn't yet know about himself but which, even in a latent state, were sufficient to have got the "opposition" all hot and worried!

EVEN IF the Guides only believed that—if they, like Knox and his mountainous registered nurse, had played around so long on the fringes of reality that they were as badly confused now as the people they'd been misleading—his intervention should still be effective! Particularly if he informed Mrs. Lovelock, with the proper degree of impressiveness, that he'd passed on the word.

A little play-acting didn't seem too much effort to put out to save a human life. Even a life like Wilson Knox's...

This time, it was Paylar who answered the telephone.

"You've disappointed me a little, Mr. Commager," she said. "When I first heard your voice, I was certain you were going to invite me out to dine and dance."

Commager assured her that this had been his primary purpose—and as soon as he'd said it, he began to wonder whether it wasn't true. But business came first, he added.

"Well, as to the business," Paylar told him demurely, "I'm not necessarily in control of Ruth's activities, you know. I hadn't been informed that the Reverend Knox was ill." She paused a moment. "I'll tell Ruth she isn't to frighten your friend again. Will that be satisfactory, Mr. Commager?"

"Why, yes, it is," Commager said and found himself flushing. Somehow, in her easy acceptance of his intervention, she'd managed to make him feel like a child whose fanciful notions were being humored by an adult. He put the idea aside, to be investigated later. "Now about where to have dinner—"

Paylar said she'd prefer to let him surprise her. "But I have a condition," she added pleasantly. "There'll be no shop-talk tonight!"

Putting him on the defensive again, Commager thought ruefully. He told her shoptalk had been far from his mind and would eight o'clock be about right?

It would be about right, she agreed. And then, arriving at the store finally, some fifteen minutes later, he found Jean Bohart waiting in his office.

"Hi, Alan," she greeted him gloomily. "You're taking me to lunch. Okay?"

In one way or another, Tuesday simply didn't look like a good day for business.

"I'M IN A mood today," Jean announced. She picked without enthusiasm at a grapefruit and watercress salad. "But you're not talking to me, either..."

"I was thinking," Commager said, "that I was glad you didn't look like a certain lady I met this morning. What's the mood about?"

She hesitated. "I'm making my mind up about something. I'll tell you tomorrow. Who was the lady? Someone I know?"

"I doubt it. A Mrs. Lovelock."

"I don't know any Lovelocks. What's the matter with her looks?"

"Fat," Commager explained.

"Well," Jean said glumly, "I'm not that."

She was, in fact, in spite of her downcast expression, a model of crisp attractiveness as usual. A white sharkskin suit, with a lavender veil gathered lightly at her throat, plus a trim white hat to one side of a blonde head—neat, alert and healthy-looking as an airline hostess, Commager thought approvingly.

Jean mightn't care for the comparison, though, so he didn't tell her. And he wasn't going to press her about the mood. At the rare moments that she became reserved, probing made her sullen. Probably something to do with Ira again.

"I called off the Taylors for tomorrow," she told him suddenly, with some traces of embarrassment, "so we could talk. You don't mind, do you?"

"Of course not," Commager said hesitantly. Then it struck him suddenly: they'd had a date for an all-day fishing party Wednesday, Jean and he and the Taylor couple. He'd forgotten completely!

"That's all right then," Jean said, looking down at her plate. She still seemed curiously shy and Commager realized that this was no ordinary problem. "Will you sleep at your cabin tonight?"

"Sure," he said, concerned—he was very fond of Jean. His sleeping at the cabin was the usual arrangement on such occasions; he'd have everything ready there for the day before anyone else arrived and then they'd be off to an early start.

"I'll be there tomorrow at eight," said Jean. She gave him a quick, unhappy smile. "I love you, Alan—you never ask questions when you shouldn't!"

SO HE HAD two dates at eight now, twelve hours apart. If it hadn't been for the attendant problems, Commager decided, his social life might have looked exceptionally well rounded at the moment to almost anybody!

But he didn't seem to be doing a very good job of keeping clear of attendant problems. It had struck him for the first time, while they were lunching, that Jean Bohart might easily have been the prototype of the figment of Lona. There were obvious general similarities, and the dissimilarities might have been his own expression of the real-life fact that Jean was Ira's wife.

But he felt himself moving into a mentally foggy area at that point. There had been occasional light lovemaking between them, too light to really count; but Jean certainly had remained emotionally absorbed with Ira, though she tended to regard him superficially with a kind of fond exasperation.

Commager didn't really know how he felt about Jean, except that he liked her more than anyone else he could think of. There was a warning awareness that if he tried to push any deeper into that particular fog right now, he might get himself emotionally snagged again.

It didn't seem advisable to become emotionally snagged. There were still too many other doubtful issues floating around.

One of the other issues resolved itself—in a way—very shortly, with the ringing of the office telephone.

It was Elaine Lovelock once more.

"Mr. Commager," she said, "about the matter we were discussing—"

He began to tell her he had spoken to Paylar, but she interrupted him: "Dr. Knox died an hour ago!"

CHAPTER EIGHT

SOME thirty minutes later, the first hot jolt of pain drove down from the center of Commager's throat to a point under the end of his breastbone.

If it hadn't been so damned pat, he thought, he might have yelled for a doctor. The sensations were thoroughly convincing.

There was a section at the back of the store devoted to the experimental breeding of fish that were priced high enough to make such domestic arrangements worthwhile and exceptionally delicate in their requirements for propagation. The section had a door that could be locked, to avoid disturbances. Commager went in and locked it.

In the swampy, hothouse atmosphere, he leaned against one of the tank racks, breathing carefully. The pain was still there, much less substantial than it had been in the first few moments, but still a vertical, hard cramping inside his chest. It had shocked him. It still did. But he was not nearly so much alarmed as angry.

The anger raged against himself—he was doing this! The suggestion to do it might have been implanted, but the response wasn't an enemy from outside, a phantom tiger pressing cold, steely claws down through his chest. It was a self-generated thing that used his own muscles, his own nerves, his own brain…

It tightened suddenly again. Steel-hard, chilling pain, along with a bitter, black, strangling nausea in his throat. "I'm doing it!" he thought.

The clamping agony was part of himself; he had created it, structured it, was holding it there now.

AND SO HE relaxed it again. Not easily, because the other side of himself, the hidden, unaware, responsive side was being stubborn. It knew it was supposed to die now, and it did its determined best.

But degree by degree, he relaxed the cramping, the tightness, and then suddenly felt it dissolve completely.

Commager stood, his legs spread apart, swaying a little drunkenly. Sweat ran from his body. His head remained cocked to the right as if listening, sensing, while he breathed in long, harsh gasps that slowed gradually.

It was gone.

And now, he thought, let's really test this thing! Let's produce it again.

That wasn't easy either, because he kept cringing in fear of its return.

But he produced it.

And this time it wasn't too hard to let it go, to let it dissolve again.

He brought it up briefly once more, a single sharp stab—and washed it away.

And that, he thought, was enough of that kind of game. He'd proved his point.

He stripped off his shirt and hosed cold water over his head and shoulders and arms. He dabbed himself with a towel, put his wet shirt back on, combed his hair and went back to the office.

Sitting there, he thought of an old gag about a moronic wrestler who, practicing holds and grips all by himself, broke his left foot and remarked admiringly, "Jeez, boss, nobody but me could have done that to me, huh?"

Which more or less covered what had happened. And now that he had made that quite clear to himself, it seemed safe to wonder whether just possibly there mightn't have been some direct, immediate prompting from outside—something that told him to go ahead and break himself apart, just as the wrestler had done.

THOUGH there needn't have been anything as direct as a telepathic suggestion. It could also have been done, quite as purposefully, by inducing the disturbed leaders of the Temple of Antique Christianity to bring their plight to his attention. By letting him become thoroughly aware of the shadowy, superstitious possibilities in the situation, opening his mind to them and their implications—and then hammering the suggestion home with the simple, indisputable fact of Wilson Knox's death!

If someone was clever enough to know Alan Commager a little better than he'd known himself so far—and had motive enough not to mind killing somebody else in order to soften him up—it could have been done in just that way. And Paylar had told him openly that the motive existed.

Commager decided that that was how it had been done; though now he didn't mind considering the possibility of a telepathic suggestion either. They might try something else, but he was quite sure that the kind of trick they had tried—whichever way it had been done—wouldn't work at all another time. They needed his cooperation for that, and he wasn't giving them any.

And still, aside from the fact that Wilson Knox had been threatened, nothing at all had occurred openly.

The anger in him remained. He couldn't bring himself to feel really sorry for Knox or for Elaine Lovelock either. They were destructive mental parasites who'd had the bad luck to run into what might be simply a more efficient parasite of the same breed. In spite of their protests, they hadn't been any less ruthless with the people they controlled.

He could recognize that. But the anger stayed with him, a smoldering and dangerous thing, a little ugly. Commager knew he was still angry with himself. For reasons still unknown, he had developed an area of soft rot in his thoughts and emotions; and he was reasonably convinced that, without that much to start on, the proddings and nibblings of parasites couldn't have had any effect. To have reduced himself to the level of becoming vulnerable to them seemed an intolerably indecent failing, like a filthy disease.

But anger, however honestly directed where it belongs, wants to strike outward.

FOR A parasite or whatever else she might be, Paylar looked flatteringly beautiful in a sheath of silver and black—and he didn't get a significant word out of her all evening.

Commager hadn't tried to talk shop, but he had expected that she would. However, in that respect it might have been simply another interesting, enjoyable, but not too extraordinary night out.

In other respects it wasn't. He didn't forget at any time that here was someone who probably shared the responsibility for what he was now rather certain had been a deliberate murder. In retrospect, her promise to tell Ruth MacDonald not to frighten Knox any more hadn't meant anything, since Knox by then had been as good as dead.

The odd thing—made much odder by the other probability that he himself had been the actual target of that killing—was that as far as Paylar was concerned he seemed unable to feel any convincing moral indignation about the event! It was puzzling enough so that, under and around their pleasant but unimportant conversation, he was mainly engaged in hunting for the cause of that lack of feeling.

Her physical attractiveness seemed involved in it somehow. Not as a justification for murder; he wasn't even so sure this evening that he liked Paylar physically. He felt the attraction, but there was also a trace of something not very far from revulsion in his involuntary response to it.

It wasn't too obvious; but she might have almost an excess of quiet vitality, a warmth and slender, soft earthiness that seemed almost more animal than human.

That thought-line collapsed suddenly. Rather, it struck Commager as if he'd been about to become aware of something he wasn't yet prepared to see.

HE SUDDENLY laughed, and Paylar's short black eyebrows lifted questioningly.

"I just worked something out, Mabel!" he explained. He'd asked her earlier what her full name was, and she had told him gravely it was Mabel Jones, and that she used Paylar for business purposes only. He didn't believe her, but, for the evening, they had settled cozily on Mabel and Alan.

"The thing that's different about you," he went on, "is that you don't have a soul. So, of course, you don't have a human conscience either!" He considered a moment. It seemed to reflect almost exactly how he felt about her. A cat was attractive, pleasant to see and to touch; and one didn't blame a cat for the squawking bird it had killed that afternoon. One didn't fairly blame a cat either if, to avenge some mysterious offense, it lashed out with a taloned paw at oneself! He developed the notion to Paylar as well as he could without violating the rule against shoptalk.

The cat-woman seemed neither amused nor annoyed at his description of her. She listened attentively and then said, "You could still join us, Alan—"

"Lady," said Commager, astonished, "there are any number of less disagreeable suggestions you could have made at this hour." He added, "Leaving out everything else, I don't like the company you keep."

Paylar shrugged naked tanned shoulders. Then her gaze went past him and froze briefly.

"What's the matter?" he inquired.

She looked back at him with a rueful smile. "I'm afraid you're going to see a little more of my company now," she remarked. "What time of night is it, Alan?"

COMMAGER checked. It was just past midnight, he told her, so it wasn't surprising that this and that should have started crawling out of the woodwork. He turned his head.

"Hello, Oracle!" he said cordially. "What do you see in the tea leaves for me?"

Ruth MacDonald looked a little out of place in a neat gray business suit. For a moment, she had also looked uncomfortably like a resurrected corpse to Commager, but she was alive enough.

She glanced at him. "I see your death," she said unsmilingly.

"You're in a bit of a rut," Commager told her. "Why don't you sit down and have a drink?"

The ice-faced young siren didn't share Paylar's immunity in his mind—she made his flesh crawl; she was something that should be stepped on...

Paylar stood up. "You're fools," she said to Ruth MacDonald without passion. She turned to Commager. "Alan, I should have told you I intended to drive back with Ruth—"

It was a lie, he thought, but he didn't mind. The expression of implacable hostility on Ruth MacDonald's face had been gratifying—Paylar's friends were becoming really unhappy about him!

The gray car stood almost at the far end of the dark parking lot where he had left his own. He walked them up to it and wished them both good night with some solemnity. "You, too, Miss MacDonald," he said, which gained him another brief glance and nothing more. Then he stepped aside to let them back out.

WHEN HE stopped moving, there was no particular psychic ability required to guess what the piece of cold metal was that was pushing against the back of his spine. "We're taking the next car," Herbert Hawkes's voice announced gently behind him. "And I'm sure we can count on you to act reasonably this time, Mr. Commager."

It was rather neat, at that. The gray car was moving slowly away, racing its engine. If there had been anyone in sight at the moment—but there wasn't—a backfire wouldn't have created any particular excitement.

"I'm a reasonable man," Commager said meekly. "Good evening, Mr. Hawkes...and you, too, Mr. Barthold. I'm to take one of the back seats, I suppose?"

"That's what we had in mind," Hawkes admitted.

They might or might not be amateurs at this kind of thing, but they didn't seem to be making any obvious mistakes. Lex Barthold was driving, and Commager sat in the seat behind him. Hawkes sat beside Barthold, half-turned toward Commager. The gun he held pointed at Commager's chest lay along the top of the backrest. From outside, if anyone happened to glance in, it would look as if the two of them were engaged in conversation.

Commager thought wistfully of his own gun, stacked uselessly away in his car. This was what came of starting to think in terms of modern witchcraft! One overlooked the simple solutions.

"I was wondering," he suggested, "what would happen if we passed a patrol-car."

Hawkes shrugged very slightly. "You might try praying that we do, Commager…"

WHETHER the possibility was bothering him or not, the big man didn't look happy. And there was a set tension about the way Lex Barthold drove that indicated an equal lack of enjoyment there. Witchcraft addicts themselves, they might feel that physical mayhem—if that was what they were contemplating—was a little out of their normal lines of activity.

Otherwise, they had brawn enough for almost any kind of mayhem, and while one needn't assume immediately that the trip was to wind up with outright murder, their attitude wasn't reassuring.

Meanwhile, he had been fascinated by the discovery that Hawkes sported a large, discolored bruise at the exact points of his neck and jaw where Commager had thought his fist had landed early Monday morning. Those "hallucinations" hadn't been entirely illusory, after all.

However, that made it a little harder again to understand what actually could have happened that night. Commager's thoughts started darting off after rather improbable explanations, such as the possibility of Ruth MacDonald's having a twin sister or a close double who had been sacrificed then—much as Knox had been—as part of the plot to drive Alan Commager out of his mind or into his grave! He shook his head. It just didn't seem very likely.

The one thing he could be sure of right now was that Hawkes, who mightn't be the most genial of men at best, hadn't appreciated that sneak punch.

They didn't pass any patrol cars…

CHAPTER NINE

HE KILLED Herbert Hawkes not a quarter of a mile away from his own Bayside cabin. The location wasn't accidental. They moved down the last fifty yards of a twisting, precipitous goat-path toward the Bay, Hawkes holding a gun on Commager all the way. Once they were past the point of possible interference, Hawkes took time out to explain.

"We're counting on your being found," he said, "and this is your own backyard, so to speak. You've gone fishing now and then from that spot down there, Commager. Tonight, being a little liquored up, you decided to go for a swim. Or you slipped and fell from all the way up here and died instantly."

Commager looked at the gun. "With a couple of bullets in me?"

"I don't think it will come to that." Both of them, in spite of Hawkes's bland analysis of the situation, were still noticeably nervous. "But if it does—well, you ran into a couple of rough characters out here, and they shot you and threw you in. Of course, we'd prefer to avoid that kind of complication."

He paused as if expecting some comment. They both stood about eight feet away, looking at Commager.

The Moon was low over the Bay, but it was big, and there was plenty of light for close-range shooting. This was a lumpy shelf of rock, not more than twenty by twenty feet, long and wide; the path dropped off to the right of it to another smaller shelf and ended presently at the water's edge, where there was a wet patch of sand when the tide was out.

The only way up from here was the path they'd come down by, and the two stood in front of that. He couldn't read Barthold's expression just now, but Hawkes was savagely tense—a big man physically confident of himself, mentally prepared for murder, but still oddly unsure and—expectant!

THE EXPLANATION struck Commager suddenly: they were wondering whether he wasn't going to produce some witchcraft trick of his own in this emergency! It was such an odd shifting of their original roles that it startled a snort of rather hysterical mirth from him; and Hawkes, in the process of handing the gun to Barthold, tried to jerk it back, and then Commager moved.

He didn't move toward Hawkes but toward Barthold, who seemed to have a better hold on the gun. They might have thought he was after it, too, because Hawkes let go and swung too hastily at him as Barthold took a step back. Commager slammed a fist into Barthold's body, swung him around between Hawkes and himself, and struck hard again. The gun didn't even go off.

He had no more time then for Barthold, because Hawkes rammed into him with disconcerting solidness and speed. In an instant, it was like fighting a baboon, all nails and muscles and smashing fists and feet. The top of Hawkes's skull butted his mouth like a rock. Commager hit him in the back of the neck, was free for a moment and hit again. Hawkes stepped back, straightening slightly, and Commager followed and struck once more, in the side. Then Hawkes disappeared.

It was as sudden as that! Realization that he was stumbling on the edge of the rock shelf himself came together with a glimpse of the thundering white commotion of surf almost vertically beneath him—a good hundred and fifty feet down.

With a terrible trembling still in his muscles, he scrambled six feet back on the shelf and glared wildly around for Lex Barthold. But his mind refused to turn away from the thought of how shockingly close he had come to going over with Hawkes; so a number of seconds passed before he grasped the fact that Barthold also was nowhere in sight.

COMMAGER'S breathing had slowed gradually, while he stared warily up the trail to the left. The noise of the water would have covered any sounds of either stealthy withdrawal or approach; but since Barthold seemed to have preferred to take himself and the gun out of the fight, it was unlikely he would be back.

On the other hand, there were a number of points on that path where he could wait for Commager to come within easy range, while he remained out of immediate physical reach himself.

To the right, the trail led down. Commager glanced in that direction again and this time saw the gun where it had dropped into the loose shale of the shelf.

Lex Barthold was lying on his back among the boulders of the next shelf down, his legs higher than his head, the upper part of his body twisted slightly to one side. He had fallen only nine feet or so, but he wasn't moving. They looked at each other for a moment; then Commager safetied the gun and put it in his pocket. He went on down.

"Hawkes went over the edge," he said, still rather dazed. "What happened to you?"

Barthold grunted. "Broke my back!" He cursed Commager briefly. "But you're a dead man, too, Commager..."

"Neither of us is dead yet," Commager told him. He felt physically heavy, cold and tired. He hesitated and added, "I'm going to go and get help for you."

Barthold shook his head slowly. "You won't get back up there alive. We've made sure of you this time..." He sounded matter-of-factly certain of it, and if he felt any concern about what would happen now to himself, there was no trace of it in his voice.

Commager stared down at him for a moment wondering, and then looked around.

SURF CRASHED rhythmically below them; the Moon seemed to be sliding fast through clouds far out over the Bay. Overhead, the broken, sloping cliffs might conceal anything or anybody. The feeling came strongly to him then that in this savage and lonely place anything could happen without affecting the human world at all or being noticed by it.

The night-lit earth seemed to shift slowly and giddily about him and then steadied again, as if he had, just then, drifted far beyond the boundaries of the reality he knew and was now somewhere else, in an area that followed laws of its own, if it followed any laws at all.

When he looked at Barthold again, he no longer felt the paradoxical human desire to find help for a man who had tried to kill him and whom he had nearly killed. He could talk in Barthold's own terms.

He bent over him. "What makes you so sure your friends have got me?"

Barthold gave him a mocking glance, but he didn't answer.

They weren't certain, Commager thought, straightening up. They were just hoping again. That something was preparing against him was an impression he'd gained himself, almost like the physical sensation of a hostile stirring and shifting in the air and the rocks about him, a secretive gathering of power. But they weren't certain...

"I think," he said slowly, "that I'll walk away from here when I feel like it." He paused, and added deliberately, "You people might last longer if you didn't try to play rough, Barthold. Except, of course, with someone like Wilson Knox."

BARTHOLD spoke with difficulty. "The reason you're still alive is that Paylar and I were the only ones who would believe you were a natural of the new mind. The first one here in twenty-three years—" His breath seemed to catch; his face twisted into a grimace of pain. "But tonight they all know that ordinary controls won't work on you, Commager. That's what makes it too late for you."

Commager hesitated. He said gently, "When did you and Paylar discover I was a natural of the new mind?"

"Sunday night, of course." Barthold was plainly anxious now to keep him here. He hurried on. "The mistake was made five years ago. You should have been destroyed then, before you had learned anything, not placed under control."

Commager's eyes widened slightly. Until that statement, he had given only a fraction of conscious attention to what Barthold was saying, the greater part of his mind alert to catch those wispy, not-quite-physical indications that something unhealthy was brewing nearby in the night. But five years ago!

"Paylar made me an offer to join your group," he pointed out. "Wouldn't that have been satisfactory?"

Barthold stared up at him. His mouth worked, but for a few seconds he made no audible reply.

"Don't wait!" he said with startling, savage intensity. "Now, or..." The words thickened and slurred into angry, incomprehensible mutterings. The eyelids closed.

Commager bent down and prodded Barthold's shoulder with a forefinger. The man might be dying—those last words hadn't sounded as if they were addressed to him—but there were things he had to know now. "What are you, Barthold? Aren't you a natural, too?"

Barthold's eyes opened and rolled toward him, but remained unpleasantly unfocused. "Old mind—" the thick voice mumbled. And then clearly, "You're a fool, Commager! You didn't really know anything. If the others..."

The eyes closed again.

Old mind... That still told him nothing. "Are the others of the old mind?"

Barthold grinned tiredly. "Why don't you ask Hawkes?"

There was a sound behind Commager like the sloshing of water in the bottom of a boat. Then he had spun around and was on his feet, his hair bristling.

HAWKES stood swaying in the moonlight, twenty feet away. Water ran from his clothes to the rocks among which he stood. Water had smeared his hair down over his face. And the left side of his head looked horribly flattened.

He took a step forward, and then came on in a swaying rush.

For a long instant of time, Commager only stared. Hawkes was dead, quite obviously, even now as he moved, he was dead—so he hadn't come climbing back up the rocks out of the sweeping tug of the waves! He—

He was gone.

Commager walked over to the point where he had seen Hawkes. The rocks were dry. He went back to Barthold, his lips still stiff with horror.

"Tell me what this was!" he said hoarsely. "Or I'll kill you now!"

Barthold was still grinning, his eyes open and wickedly alert. "A picture I let you look at—but, you see, you learn too fast. You're a natural. You wouldn't believe a picture now, and the old mind couldn't do anything else to you. But there are others working for us—and now—"

There was a rumbling and a grinding and a rushing sound overhead. Commager leaped back, his eyes darting up. He heard Lex Barthold screaming.

The whole upper cliff-side was moving, sliding downward. A gray-black, turning, almost vertical wave of broken rock dropping toward them...

CHAPTER TEN

"PEOPLE like us," Jean Bohart remarked, with an air of moody discovery, "are really pretty lucky!"

Commager went "Hm?" drowsily. Then he lifted his head to look at her. She stood beside the Sweet Susan's lashed wheel, shaded blue eyes gazing at him from under the brim of her yachting cap, hands clasped behind her. "What brought that to mind?" he inquired.

"I was thinking about my troubles," she said. "Then I started thinking they weren't really so bad! Comparatively—"

She was keeping her voice light. Commager sat up from where he'd stretched himself out beside the cabin, gathering his thoughts back out of the aimless diffusion of sleep. "Ready to talk about your troubles now?"

Jean shook her head. "Not yet." She frowned. "There's something about them I want to figure out by myself first— and I'm not quite done." The frown vanished. "If you've finished your nap, you might look around and see what a grand morning it is! That's what I meant by being lucky."

They were off Dana Point, he saw, so he'd slept a full hour since Jean had taken them out of the Newport Beach harbor. The Sweet Susan was running smoothly southward, through the Pacific's long smooth swells. Now that he was sitting up, the wind streamed cool about his head and neck and shoulders.

He said, "Yes, I guess we're lucky."

Jean grinned. "And since I've got you awake, I'll catch a nap myself! Not that I spent the night boozing and brawling."

Commager smiled at her. "Any time you feel like putting in a night like that, give me a ring."

Superficially, in her white slacks and thin sweater, Jean Bohart looked fresh as a daisy; only the tautness about her mouth and a controlled rigidity in the way she stood suggested that the "trouble" might be close to a complete emotional disaster.

He'd thought earlier that he would have liked to get out of this jaunt if he could; now he felt guilty and a little alarmed.

HE MOVED over near the wheel while she lay down on the bench, pulling a pillow under her head and settling back with the cap-brim down over her eyes. He could tell that the muscles of the slim straight body weren't actually going to relax. But she would pretend now to be asleep and Commager let his thoughts shift away from Jean, promising himself to give her his full attention as soon as she was ready to talk.

There were a few problems of his own to be considered, though at the moment he had the sense of a truce, a lull. Last night, he had shaken the Guides badly; he had killed two of their members. But there were at least three left, and he hadn't crippled their power to act.

The truce, if it was that, was due in part to their fear of his reaction and in part to an entirely different kind of restraint— a restraint which he believed was self-imposed.

The reason he believed it was that he was now aware of being under a similar restraint himself. He thought he knew why it was an inescapable limitation, but impersonally he could agree with Paylar's opinion that, from the Guides' point of view, he should have been destroyed as soon as they became aware of him.

Left to himself—if in curiosity he had begun to investigate PSI—he would have discovered the limitation quickly enough and abided by it. Even so, it appeared to permit an enormously extended range of effective activity. And Barthold had implied a conflict between an "old mind" and a "new mind."

It sounded like an esoteric classification of varying degrees of human PSI potential—an ascendant individual "new mind" threatening the entrenched and experienced but more limited older group, which compensated for its limitation by bringing functioning members of the "new mind" under its control or repressing or diverting their developing abilities.

He apparently was a "natural of the new mind." He couldn't be permanently controlled. To the older group he represented an intolerable threat.

SOMEONE last night had thrown a few thousand tons of stone at him! And he had deflected that missile from its course. Not by very much, but just enough to keep it clear of the frantically scrambling figure of himself, scuttling up the cliff path like a scared beetle.

He had done it—how?

Trying to restructure the action, Commager knew that the process itself hadn't been a conscious one. But it had been symbolized in his awareness by a cluster of pictures that took in the whole event simultaneously.

A visualization of himself and the long thundering of the rocks, the sideward distortion of their line of fall, and a final picture again of himself as he reached the top of the cliff unharmed.

It had all been there in a momentary, timeless swirling of possibilities against the background of rock and shadow, the tilted, turning sky and moonlight glittering on racing waters.

Then, in an instant, the pattern had been set, decided on; and the event solidified into reality with the final thudding crash. Barthold lay buried under the rocks and perhaps, down in the water, the body of Hawkes also had been caught and covered.

He hadn't tried to save Barthold. Instead he had automatically flung out another kind of awareness, a flashing search for the mind that had struck at him. And he had been prepared, in a way he couldn't have described now, to strike back.

He "found" three of them—the one who had acted and two who merely observed. Almost, not quite, he knew where they were. But they were alert. It was as if something barely glimpsed had been flicked out of his sight, leaving a lifeless black emptiness for him to grope through if he chose.

Commager didn't choose to do any blind groping. He wasn't sure enough of himself for that.

THE LIMITATION that he—and apparently they—didn't dare to violate had to do with the preservation of appearances. It was a line of thought he didn't want to follow too far just now. But it seemed that the reality he knew and lived in was a framework of appearances, tough and durable normally, but capable of being distorted into possibly chaotic variations.

The penalty seemed to be that to the degree one distorted the framework, he remained distorted himself. The smooth flow of appearances was quickly re-established, but the miracle-worker found himself left somehow outside. Commager suspected that he stayed outside.

He suspected also that a really significant distortion of appearances would thrust the life and mind that caused it so far out that, for all practical purposes, it ceased to exist.

He wasn't tempted to test the theory. Its apparent proof was that reality by and large did remain intact, while those who played around too consistently with even minor infringements notoriously failed to thrive.

To let a pair of dice briefly defy the laws of chance probably did no harm to anyone, but when you aimed and launched the side of a cliff as a missile of murder, you were very careful that the result was a rockslide and not a miracle!

You didn't—ever—disturb the world of reality.

WHAT HE had to fear from them, if they broke the truce, was the ambush, the thing done secretly under the appearance of a natural series of events. It left an unpleasantly large number of possibilities open, but until something new happened, he couldn't know that they weren't ready to call it a draw. So far his spontaneous reactions had been entirely effective. The obvious damage was all on the other side.

But since the damage wasn't all obvious, he had no present intention of forcing a showdown. "Natural" or not, he might be either not quite good enough at that kind of game, or much too good.

But meanwhile Commager looked thoughtfully at Jean Bohart. She had fallen asleep finally, but she wasn't sleeping comfortably. Her mouth moved fretfully, and she made small whimpering sounds from time to time, almost like a puppy that is dreaming badly. If he'd become a miracle-worker on a small scale, Commager thought, if he'd already pushed himself to some degree beyond the normal limits of reality, he might as well get some use out of what he couldn't undo.

Looking at her, it wasn't too difficult to imagine the rigidities and tensions that kept Jean from finding any real physical rest. Nor was it hard to get a picture of her emotional disturbances shaping themselves into a scurrying and shifting dream-torment.

Carefully, Commager took hold of the two concepts. He waited until he could no longer be quite sure whether it was he or Jean who was really experiencing these things; and then, as he had done yesterday with the pain in his own body, he let dreams and tensions ebb away and cease to be.

In spite of everything else that had happened, he was still amazed, a few moments later, to realize that his experiment in therapy had been a complete success.

CHAPTER ELEVEN

CLEAR BLUE bowl of the sky above. Black-blue choppy water of the Pacific all about. The Sweet Susan drifted, throttled down and almost stationary. Near the kelp beds two miles to the south, eight other boats gradually changed their relative positions. In the northeast, toward which the Sweet Susan slowly moved, the dark jaws of the Bay opened out, still too far off to make out the scars of last night's rock-slide.

Jean had slept steadily for over an hour, and Commager had two lines trailing under superficial observation. Not even a mackerel had taken any interest so far, which probably wasn't due to the sinister influence of the Guides, but to the fact that the deep drop outside the Bay simply wasn't a very good fishing area.

Unconcerned about that, he'd been sitting there for some while, in a drowsy, sun-bright daydream composed of an awareness of physical well-being, his odd certainty that the truce still held, and enjoyment of the coincidence that the Sun was getting hotter to the exact degree that the breeze got brisker in compensation. For the hour, under such circumstances, the life of an unambitious, healthy animal seemed to be about as much as anybody reasonably could ask for.

He came out of it with a sort of frightened start. He had heard Jean stirring on the bench behind him. Now she yawned just audibly and sat up, and he knew she was looking at him.

Commager couldn't have said what kept him from turning his head. There was a momentary questioning alarm in him, which stiffened into cold watchfulness as Jean got up and went into the cabin. There had been another little shift in the values of reality while he was off-guard, he thought. Something was a shade wrong again, a shade otherwise than it had been an hour or so ago. But he didn't yet know what it was.

INA MINUTE or so Jean came out again, and he guessed she'd changed into her swimsuit. He heard her come up behind him, and then a pair of smooth arms were laid lightly across his shoulders and a voice, from a point a little above and behind his head, inquired, "Had any luck, Alan? The Sun got a bit too hot for me."

It shocked him completely because it was Lona who touched him and spoke.

It was also, of course, Jean Bohart—and there was no longer any question that she'd served as the model for his imaginary woman. It had been out of just such scraps of illusion as this—voice sounds and touches, distorted seconds in time—that he'd built up that self-deception.

How he had been reached in the first place to get him started on the construction was something he couldn't yet recall, but the purpose was also completely obvious.

Five years ago, Lex Barthold had said, they'd taken him under control.

To divert a mind from a direction you didn't want it to follow, you gave it a delusion to stare at.

You drenched the delusion in violently unpleasant emotions, which kept the mind from any closer investigation of the disturbance...

Apparently, they'd expected the treatment to be effective for the rest of his lifetime. But when Ira reported on the minor sensation Commager had created in a Las Vegas club, they'd come alert to the fact that his developing PSI abilities hadn't been permanently stunted. And then a majority of them had been afraid to attempt to kill a "natural."

Unconsciously, he'd resisted the next maneuver—drastic as it had been—to throw him into a delusive tizzy.

Then he'd begun to strike back at them.

It wasn't really surprising, he thought, that they'd become a little desperate. And they might have known of that dice game before Ira told them about it. Ira had been their means of contacting him directly.

As Jean had been the means of keeping the primary delusion reinforced and alive.

"NO LUCK, so far!" he told her, somewhat carefully. The momentary shock of recognition had faded, but some of the feeling he'd wasted on the delusion seemed to have transferred itself back to the model now! It didn't really surprise him, and it wasn't an unpleasant sensation; but for a moment at least, he didn't want it to show in his voice. "Did you get caught up on your sleep?"

It might have showed in his voice, because she moved away from him and leaned over the side of the boat, looking at the lines. "Uh-huh!" she said casually. "I feel fine now! Better than I have in a long time, as a matter of fact."

Commager regarded her speculatively. The easy grace of her body confirmed what she said; the tensions were gone. He patted himself mentally on the back. Commager the Healer!

"Alan?"

"Yes?" he said.

"I'm leaving Ira." Her face flushed a little. "To be more exact about it, Ira's leaving me. For that MacDonald woman you met Sunday."

"I'll be damned..." Commager said softly. His thoughts were racing as she went on.

"He told me yesterday morning. It jolted my vanity, all right. But the funny thing is that as soon as I got over it, I found I actually didn't care. It was really a relief. Isn't that funny?"

He didn't think it was funny. It was a little too pat.

"FOR FIVE years," she said, turning to face him, "I thought I loved that guy. And now I find I never did..." She shook her head. "I don't get it, Alan. How can anyone be so crazy?"

"What are you going to do?" he asked.

She stared at him for a moment, looking appealing, hurt and lovely. If he put his hand out to her now, she'd be in his arms.

"I'm going to Florida for a few months. Ira can settle it any way he wants to."

So that was the way it had been, Commager thought in astounded fury. He was the one they'd wanted to hold down, but it wasn't only his life they'd twisted and distorted to do it. They'd used Jean just as ruthlessly. And, perhaps, Ira—

For five years, he could have had his imaginary woman. She'd been within his reach in reality.

And, now that delusions were not working so well any more, they threw the reality at him!

Only now it was a little too late. He'd changed too far to be able to accept their gift.

"Jean," he said.

"Yes, Alan?"

"You're going to stop thinking, for a while now," he told her gently. "You're going to just stand there for a while and not be aware of anything that happens."

A puzzled frown formed on her face as he started to speak, but it smoothed out again, and then she went on looking placidly at him. Perhaps her eyes had dulled a trifle.

THIS TIME, it didn't surprise Commager at all. Out beyond the Sweet Susan, he saw something like a faint haze beginning to shape itself over the moving surface of the water. He grinned a little.

Slowly and deliberately, he framed the cold thought in his mind: *Do what you can for yourselves! The truce is over!*

Their response was an instantaneous one. A long swell rose up behind the Sweet Susan, lifted the boat, passing beneath it, and dropped it again. The Sweet Susan was still rising as Commager picked up Jean Bohart and set her down beside the bench near the wheel; and it slapped down in a smash of spray as he cut the lashings of the wheel with the emergency knife and pulled out the throttle.

He glanced around. The haze was a thick fog about them, brilliant white against the blue of the sky overhead, while they ran through its wet, gray shade. The boat shuddered sideways behind the big swell, water roiling about it. Suddenly, with a kind of horror, Commager understood what was there.

He had seen pictures of it, or rather of a part of it, cast up on the coast years before: a house-sized chunk of rotten, oddly coarse-grained flesh, hurriedly disposed of and never identified. The drifted remnant of a nameless phenomenon of the Pacific deeps.

The phenomenon itself was underneath them now!

STILL TOO far down to have done more than briefly convulse the surface as it turned, it was rising toward the boat. A thing of icy, incredible pressures, it was disrupted and dying as it rose, incapable of understanding the impulse that had forced it from the dark ocean up toward the coast hours before. But it was certain that, in the bright glare above it, it would find and destroy the cause of its pain.

So it came up with blind, hideous swiftness; and Commager discovered that rushing bulk could not be simply turned away from them as he had turned the rocks. It was driven by its own sick and terrible purpose. Neither could he reach the minds that guided it. This time, they were alertly on guard.

With seconds to spare then, he turned the boat.

In the fog to their left, the sea opened in a thundering series of crashes and settled again. Water smashed into the boat as it danced and drove raggedly away, and before it had gone very far it was lifted once more on a thrust of water from below.

The thing from the sea had followed, and it was terribly close! So close that the flickering dull glow of a mind as primitive as the monstrous body itself rose up in Commager's awareness.

He caught at it.

What he drove into the glow was like an insistence on its destruction. It seemed to blaze up in brief, white fury and then went black...

The Sweet Susan drove on through a curiously disturbed sea, surrounded by dissipating wisps of what might or might not have been an ordinary patch of fog. Probably, no one on any of the distant fishing boats even noticed that minor phenomenon.

A half-mile away, the water roiled once more; and that was all. The Pacific had gone back to its normal behavior.

CHAPTER TWELVE

IT WAS sunset on the Bay, and Paylar was talking, at least most of the time. Sometimes Commager listened and sometimes he didn't.

It was a fairy tale situation he thought, somewhat amused at himself. Because he could feel the mood of it very strongly, a childlike one, a mood of enchantment around him and of terror along the fringes of the enchantment. Terror that was in part past, and in part still to come.

Far below the slope where they sat, sun-fires gleamed in the dark, moving waters, like fire shining out of the heart of a black jewel. Down there, as was not inappropriate near the end of a fairy tale, two of the bad ones lay dead and buried, unless one of them had been taken away by the water.

Much farther out, miles out, the body of a defeated dragon bumped slowly along the sea bottom, back to the deeps, nibbled at, tugged at, pulled and turned by armies of hungry fish.

A blonde and beautiful princess was halfway to the far land of flowers called Florida by now, flying through the night skies, and released at last from an evil enchantment. She might still wonder at how oddly she'd acted the past few years, but she'd begun to look forward to new and exciting activities—and she was rapidly forgetting Alan Commager in the process.

It had been the only way to arrange it, because this was a trap of magic Jean had no business being in, and she'd been in it only because of him. He'd got himself the other one, the dark, beautiful, wicked witch, to keep company instead.

So Paylar talked of magical things and he listened, pleasantly fascinated and willing for an hour to believe anything she told him. Earth turned under them, vast and ponderous, away from the Sun and into the night, a big, convincing stage background to what she was talking about.

ALL EARTH life, she said, was a single entity, growing and developing from this great globe, and its conscious thinking processes went on mainly in that part of it that was human. Which was fine, she explained, while all humans were still Old Mind, as they had been at first, because they were aware of Earth and cared for it, knowing they were a part of it, and that it all belonged together. But then New Mind humans came along as a natural development. They could think a little better than the others, but they were no longer aware of being a part of Earth life and didn't care about anything much but themselves, since they considered themselves to be individuals.

It didn't matter too much. They were still influenced by the purpose and patterns of Earth life, and had practically no conscious defenses against what seemed to them to be obscure motivations of their own. And there were always enough Old Mind people around who knew what was going on to direct the rather directionless New Minders patiently back to the old patterns, so that in the long run things tended to keep moving along much as they always had done.

It began to matter when New Minders developed a conscious interest in what was now called PSI. That was an Earth life ability that had its purpose in keeping the patterns intact; and only the New Mind, which had intelligence without responsibility, was capable of using PSI individualistically and destructively.

In most periods of time, the New Mind was kept from investigating PSI seriously by its superstitious dread of phenomena it couldn't rationalize. But when it did get interested—

In the Old Mind, adherence to the Earth life pattern was so complete that dangerous PSI abilities simply didn't develop.

"So you see," she said, "we need New Mind PSI to control New Mind PSI."

COMMAGER said he'd come to understand that finally. And also that they were able to keep control of the people they used by the fact that PSI abilities tended to be as deadly to their possessor as to anyone else, when employed without careful restraint. "At best, I imagine there's a high turnover rate in the New Mind section of an organization like the Guides."

"There is," she agreed coolly. "Particularly since we select the ones that are potentially the most dangerous as recruits. The ones most hungry for power. Ruth, for example, is not likely to live out another year."

Privately and thoughtfully, Commager confirmed that opinion. "Doesn't that unusual mortality attract attention?" he inquired. It seemed a little tactless, but he added, "What about Hawkes and Barthold, for example? Aren't they going to be officially missed?"

"Hawkes was known to be nearly psychopathic," Paylar replied. "Whatever happened to him will surprise no one officially. And no one but ourselves knew anything about Lex."

She had showed, Commager thought, an appalling indifference to the fate of her late companions. He studied her for a moment with interested distaste. "You know," he remarked then, "I don't feel any very strong urges for power myself. How does that fit in with your story?"

She shrugged. "A natural is always unpredictable. You have a blend of Old Mind and New Mind qualities, Alan, that might have made you extremely useful to us. But since you didn't choose to be useful, we can't take a chance on you."

He let that pass. "Where do people like you and Barthold come from?" he inquired curiously. "How did you get involved in this kind of thing?"

SHE HERSELF came from a mountain village in northern Italy. Its name was as unimportant as her own. As for the role she was playing, in part she'd been instructed in it, and in part she'd known instinctively what she had to do. She smiled at him. "But none of that is going to concern you very much longer, Alan."

She sounded unpleasantly certain about it. Although he thought he could foretell quite precisely what was going to happen tonight, Commager felt a little shaken. He suggested, "What would happen if people like myself were just left to do as they pleased?"

"Earth would go insane," she said calmly. The extravagance of the statement jolted him again, but he could see the analogue. The Old Mind was full of fears, too—the fear of chaos.

"That offer you made me to become one of the Guides— was that a trap, or was it meant sincerely?"

Her face abruptly became cautious and alert. "It was meant sincerely."

"How could you have trusted me?"

She said evasively, "There was a great deal you could have learned from us. You have discovered some of the things you can do by yourself, but you realize the dangers of uninstructed experimentation."

He looked at her, remembering the limitations of Old Mind and that because of them there couldn't be any real compromise. He didn't doubt they would have showed him what was safe to do and of use to them; but the only circumstances under which they really could trust him would be to have him so befuddled that he'd be almost completely dependent on their assistance and advice. So they would also have showed him things that were very much less than safe— for him.

He thought that Herbert Hawkes had followed that road almost to the end before he died, and that Ruth MacDonald was rather far advanced on it by now. Those two had been merely greedy and power-hungry people, utilizing talents that were more expensive than they'd been allowed to guess. Lex and Paylar had been the only leaders among the ones he'd met of that group.

He didn't bother to repeat his question; but Paylar said suddenly, "Why did you bring me out here this evening, Alan?"

"I THOUGHT I might find what was left of the Guides at Hawkes' place," Commager said. "I was a little annoyed, frankly, both because of something that happened today, and because of something that was done a while ago to somebody else. I was going to tell you to stop playing games around me and people I happen to like—or else!" He grinned at her. "Of course, I realized you weren't going to risk a showdown right in the middle of town. It could get a little too spectacular. But since you were conveniently waiting alone there for me, I brought you out here."

"Supposing," Paylar said, "that we don't choose to accept a showdown here either?"

"Lady," he told her, "if it looks as if nothing is going to be settled, there are experiments I can start on with you that should have you yelling very quickly for help to any Guides remaining in the area. As I figure it, you see, a New Mind natural might be able to control an Old Mind expert very much as you intended to control me."

She went a little white. "That could be true. But you can't hope to survive a showdown, Alan…"

He spread his hands. "Why not? Logically, at least, I don't think there are very many of you left." He was almost certain he knew of one who hadn't openly played a part as yet, but he didn't intend to mention that name at the moment. "It wouldn't take more than a handful of developed New Mind PSIs to control an area like this. And you wouldn't want more than a handful around or you couldn't be sure of controlling them."

She nodded. "That's also true, of course. But you're still at a hopeless disadvantage, Alan. We—the Old Mind knows exactly how this situation can be resolved in our favor, if we're prepared to lose a few more of our controlled PSIs…"

"The PSIs mightn't feel quite so calm about it," Commager pointed out. He hesitated. "Though I suppose you might have them believing by now that I'm out to eat them…"

"They've been led to consider you a deadly threat to their existence," Paylar agreed with a touch of complacency. "They'll take any risk that's required, particularly since they won't understand the full extent of the risk. And that isn't all, Alan. You're not the first New Mind natural we've dealt with, you know. If anything goes seriously wrong in this area, Old Mind all over the Earth will be aware of it."

HE FROWNED doubtfully at her, because he'd been wondering about that. And then he let the thought come deliberately into the foreground of his consciousness that he would prefer to reach an agreement, if it could be done. The Guides' ability to grasp what was going on in his mind seemed to be a very hazy one; but in a moment, though

Paylar's expression didn't change, he was certain she had picked up that intentional piece of information.

She said, with a slow smile, "How much do you remember of your parents, Alan?"

He stared at her in surprise. "Not very much. They both died when I was young. Why?"

She persisted. "Do you recall your mother at all?"

"No," he admitted warily. "She divorced my father about two years after I was born. I stayed with him and never saw her again. I understand she died about three years later."

"And your father?" she asked him insistently.

Commager gestured patiently toward the Bay. "My father drowned out there on a fishing trip when I was eleven. I remember him well enough, actually. Afterward I was raised by a guardian. Do you mind telling me what these questions are about?"

"Your father," she said, "was of the Old Mind, Alan. So he must have known what you might develop into almost since your birth."

ODDLY ENOUGH he found he was immediately willing to accept this as valid information. "Why didn't he do something about his shocking little offspring?" he inquired.

"Apparently," Paylar said calmly, "he did. If he hadn't died, your special abilities might have been blocked away so completely that they would never have come to your attention—or brought you to our attention. As it was, what he did to check you was simply not sufficient."

Commager considered the possibility, and again it seemed that that was what had occurred. It was too long ago to arouse any particular emotion in him. He said absently, watching her, "What's all this supposed to prove, Paylar?"

"That we're not trying to control you out of malice. It seems as necessary to us now as it did to your father then."

He shrugged. "That makes no difference, you know. If more control is all you have to offer, I'm afraid we'll go right on disagreeing."

Paylar nodded. Then she just sat there, apparently unconcerned, apparently satisfied with what had been said and with things as they were, until Commager added suddenly, "I get the notion that you've just informed your little pals it's time for direct action. Correct?"

"Two of them are on their way here." She gave him her slight smile. "When they arrive, we'll see what occurs. Would you like me to show you some pictures meanwhile?"

"Pictures?" He stared at her and laughed. He was baffled and also quite furious. He could, as she must realize and as he had once threatened to do, break her slim neck in one hand. The indications were that he could break her mind as easily if he exerted himself in that direction. But she seemed completely unconcerned about either possibility.

HER SMILE widened. "I caught that," she remarked. "You were really broadcasting, Alan! You won't try to hurt me. You're really incapable of it—unless you become very frightened. And you're almost sure you can handle all three of us anyway, so you're not yet afraid..."

And in that, for once, she might have given him more information than she knew. Because he had sensed there had been three of them involved, two actively and one as an observer, in the last two attempts against him. Paylar, he guessed, had been the observer—supervisor might be the better term.

If those three were the only Guides that remained active locally, she was quite right; he was convinced he could handle them. And if, as seemed likely, they were going to leave him no choice about it, he would.

What Old Mind elsewhere might think or do would be another matter then. He wasn't at all sure that he couldn't handle that problem also. Another piece of information Paylar had given him in the last minute or so was that sudden flares of emotion made him "legible" to "those who had her own level of ability."

He would avoid such emotional outbursts in future.

"What kind of pictures did you intend to show me?" he inquired.

"You think I'm trying to trap you," she accused him.

"Aren't you?" Commager asked, surprised.

"Of course! But only by showing you what Earth-life really is like—while there is still time."

"Well," he said agreeably, "go ahead…"

SO HE SAT there in the dark between sunset and moonrise and watched pictures, though that wasn't quite what they were. At first it seemed as if time were flowing around him; the Moon would be overhead briefly and gone again, while the planes of the ground nearby shifted and changed. That, he thought, was to get him used to the process, condition him a little. The trickeries would come next!

But when they came, they weren't really trickery. He was simply being shown life as Old Mind knew it, though he himself had never thought to take quite so dramatic and vivid a view of it. Laughing and crying, thundering and singing, Earth-life drifted past in terrors and delights, flows of brightness and piercing sound and of blackest silence and night.

At last, through all that tumult of light and fragrance and emotion, he began to grow aware of what to Old Mind was primarily there: the driving, powerful, unconscious but tremendous purpose. Earth dying and living, near-eternal…

In his mind, he found himself agreeing that it was a true picture of life and a good one.

He was a traitor to that life, Old Mind whispered to him. Earth needed him and had created him to help hold back the night and the cold forever! But the tiny, individual selfishness of the New Mind broke away from the flow of life and denied it.

So, in the end, all would die together—

The flow slowed. Into it crept the cold and the dark—a chill awareness of the approaching frozen and meaningless immobility of chaos.

It wasn't till then that Commager reached out carefully and altered the pictures a trifle. It had been a good show, he thought, though overly dramatic; and Paylar had timed the paralyzing emergence of chaos very nicely. The two for whom he'd been waiting had just reached the turnoff from the highway.

CHAPTER THIRTEEN

THE HEADLIGHTS of the car glided swiftly down the Bay Road, as he brought his awareness back hurriedly to his immediate surroundings to check on the physical condition of his companion. She sat upright a few feet away from him, her legs crossed under her, her hands dropped laxly into her lap, while the black animal eyes stared in blind horror at the frozen picture of chaos.

She would keep, he decided. And he wasn't really worried about the other two...Ira Bohart and Ruth MacDonald.

He reached out for them, and as they flashed savagely back at him, he drew away, out of time, into the space that was open to New Mind only, where they would have to follow if they wanted to touch him.

They followed instantly, with a furious lust for destruction, which wasn't unexpected but which shocked him nevertheless. They came like daggers of thought, completely reckless, and if they succeeded in touching him in the same way he had touched the sea-thing, the struggle would be over in an instant.

It became obvious immediately that he could prevent them from doing it, which—since he was a stronger, more fully developed specimen of their own class—was only to be expected. What concerned him was their utter lack of consideration for their own survival. The car they were in hadn't stopped moving; in less than half a minute now it would be approaching the sharp curve above the Bay.

He had counted on the driver's attention being forced away from him momentarily, either to stop the car or to manipulate it safely around the curve; in that instant, he would bring the other one under his control as completely as he had trapped Paylar, and he would then be free to deal at his leisure with the driver.

INDIVIDUALLY, any one of the Guides was weaker than a New Mind natural; it had looked as simple as that! He wanted to save what was left of the group, to operate through them very much as Old Mind had been doing, but with a very different purpose.

The two who attacked should be withdrawing by now, dismayed at not having found him paralyzed by Paylar's "pictures," as they must have expected. They might be waiting for her to come to their assistance in some other manner, not knowing that she was no longer even aware of the struggle. However, within seconds the need of controlling the car would become urgent enough to settle the issue—

In an instant, he felt himself drawn down, blinded and smothered, in the grasp of a completely new antagonist! It was not so much the awareness of power immensely beyond that of the Guides that stunned him; it was a certainty that this new contact was a basically horrible and intolerable thing. In the fractional moment of time that everything in him was straining simply to escape from it, the New Minders drove through their attack.

Pain was exploding everywhere through his being, as he wrenched himself free. Death had moved suddenly very close! Because the third opponent wasn't Paylar, never had been Paylar. He had miscalculated—and so there had been one he'd overlooked.

Now they had met, he knew he wasn't capable of handling this third opponent and the two New Minders together.

Then without warning the New Minders vanished out of his awareness, like twin gleams of light switched off. Seconds later, from somewhere far out on the edge of his consciousness, as if someone else were thinking it, the explanation came: *The car! They weren't able to stop the car!*

With that, the last of them drove at him again; and for a moment he was swept down into its surging emotions, into a black wave of rage and terror, heavy and clinging. But he was not unprepared for it now, and he struck at the center of its life with deadly purpose, his own terrors driving him. Something like a long, thin screaming rose in his mind...

In that moment, complete understanding came.

As in a dream scene, he was looking down into the yard of the Temple of Antique Christianity. It was nighttime now; and on the dais he'd investigated the day before, a bulky, shapeless figure twisted and shook under a robe-like cloth which covered it completely.

The screaming ended abruptly, and the shape lay still.

CHAPTER FOURTEEN

COMMAGER sat up dizzily. He discovered first that he was incredibly drenched with sweat, and that Paylar still sat in an unchanged position, as she stared at the thing he'd set before her mind to fix her attention. Down on the Bay Road, there was a faint shouting.

He stood up shakily and walked forward till he could look down to the point where the road curved sharply to the left to parallel the Bay. The shouting had come from there. A few people were moving about, two of them with flashlights. Intermittently, in their beams, he could see the white, smashed guard railings.

A brief, violent shuddering overcame him, and he went back to where Paylar sat, trying to organize his thoughts. The reason for her confident expectance of his defeat was obvious now.

The unsuspected opponent—the gross shape that had kicked about and died on the dais, the woman he'd known as Mrs. Lovelock—had been another New Mind natural. Or, rather, what had become of a New Mind natural after what probably had been decades of Old Mind control! But that part wasn't the worst of it.

I met her and talked to her! he thought in a flash of grief and horror. *But I couldn't guess—*

He drove the thought from his mind. If he wanted to go on living—and he realized with a flicker almost of surprise that he very much did—he had other work to complete tonight. A kind of work that he'd considered in advance as carefully as the rest of it—

And this time, he thought grimly, he'd better not discover later that he'd miscalculated any details.

He sat down and rolled over on his side in the exact place and position in which he'd been lying before. Almost the last thing he saw was the sudden jerky motion of Paylar's body, as he dissolved the visual fixation he'd caught her attention in. Then, as she turned her head quickly to look at him, he closed his eyes.

WHEN Commager's mind resumed conscious control of his body, there was a cloudy sky overhead and a cool gray wetness in the air. Paylar stood nearby, looking thoughtfully down at him.

He looked back at her without speaking. The terrifying conviction of final failure settled slowly and dismally on him.

"You can wake up fully now," she told him. "It's nearly morning."

He nodded and sat up.

"What I shall tell you," her voice went on, "are things you will comprehend and know to be true. But consciously you will forget them again as soon as I tell you to forget. You understand?"

Commager nodded again.

"Very well," she said. "Somewhere inside you something is listening to what I am saying; and I'm really speaking now to that part of you—inside. Here and tonight, Alan, you very nearly won, though of course you could not have won in the final issue. But you must understand now, consciously and unconsciously, that you have been completely defeated. Otherwise, you would not stop struggling until you had destroyed yourself—as thoroughly as another one, very like yourself, whom you met tonight, did years ago..."

She paused. "You know, of course, that the New Mind natural you killed tonight was your mother. We counted on the shock of that discovery to paralyze you emotionally, if all else failed. When it happened, for the few seconds during which the shock was completely effective, I was released by others of their Old Mind from the trap in which you had caught me."

She smiled. "That was a clever trap, Alan! Though if it hadn't been so clever, we might not have needed to sacrifice your mother. In those few seconds, you see, I planted a single, simple compulsion into your mind—that when you pretended afterward to become unconscious—as it appeared you were planning to do to deceive the Old Mind—your consciousness actually would blank out."

HE TRIED TO remember. Something like that had occurred! He had intended to act as if the struggle with the New Minders had exhausted him to the point where it was possible for Paylar to take him under complete control, since only in that way could he be safe from continuing Old Mind hostility. But then—

He had no awareness of what had happened in the hours that followed till now!

"You see?" Paylar nodded. There was a trace of compassion, almost of regret, in her expression. "Believe me, Alan, never in our knowledge has a functioning human mind been so completely trapped as you are now. I have been working steadily on you for the past six hours, and even now it would be impossible for you to detect the manner in which you are limited. But within minutes, you will simply forget the fact that any limitations have been imposed on you, and so you will remain free of the internal conflicts that destroyed your mother."

She paused. "And here is a final proof for you, Alan, of why this was necessary for us. You recalled that your father drowned in this Bay when you were a child. But as yet you seem to have blocked out of your memory the exact manner in which he died…"

Her voice changed, grew cold and impersonal. "Let that memory come up now, Alan!"

THE MEMORY came. With it came memory of the shocking conflict of emotion that had caused him to bury the events of that day long ago. But it aroused no emotional response in him now. It had been a member of an alien, hostile species he had compelled to thrust itself down into the water, until the air exploded from its lungs and it sank away and drowned…of the same hostile species as the one talking to him now.

"Yes," she said. "You drowned him, Alan, when you first became aware of the mental controls he had imposed on you. And then you forced yourself to forget, because your human conditioning made the memory intolerable. But you aren't truly human, you see. You are—an evolutionary mistake that might destroy the life of all Earth if left unchecked!"

She concluded, "It has taken all these years to trap you again, under conditions that would permit us to impose controls that no living mind, even in theory, could break. But the efforts and the risks have been well worthwhile to Old Mind! For you see, we can use your abilities now to make sure there will be no trouble from others of your kind for many years to come. And we can, as the need arises, direct you to condition others of your kind exactly as you have been conditioned. But now…" A flat, impersonal command drove at him again through her voice. "…forget what I have told you. All of it!"

And, consciously, the mind of Commager forgot.

HE HAD DONE, he thought, as he watched his body stand up and follow the woman up the path to his cabin, a superbly complete job of it!

What identity might remain was an intriguing problem for future research, though perhaps not one that he himself would solve. For practical purposes at any rate, the identity of Alan Commager was no longer absorbed by the consciousness that rose from and operated through his brain and body.

And that was the only kind of consciousness Old Mind knew about. He was hidden from Paylar's species now because he had gone, and would remain permanently, beyond the limits of their understanding.

He directed an order to the body's mind and the body stumbled obediently, not knowing why it had stumbled. Paylar turned and caught its arm, almost solicitously, steadying it.

"You'll feel all right again after a few hours rest, Alan," she told it soothingly.

Species as alien almost as a cat or a slender, pretty monkey, but with talents and purposes of her own, Paylar was—he thought—an excellent specimen of the second highest development of Earth evolution.

He reached very carefully now through the controls he had imposed on her consciousness to the core of her being, and explained gently to her what he had done.

For a few seconds, he encountered terror and resistance, but resignation came then, and finally understanding and a kind of contentment.

She would help him faithfully against Old Mind now, though she would never be aware of doing it.

And that, he thought, was really all for the moment. The next step, the development of New Mind PSI in others, was an unhurried, long-term project. In all the area within his range, Old Mind control had stifled or distorted whatever promise originally had been present.

BUT THE abilities were ever recurring. And here and there, as he became aware of them now, their possessors would be contacted, carefully instructed and shielded against Old Mind spies. Until they had developed sufficiently to take care of themselves and of others. Until there were enough of them.

Enough to step into the role for which they had been evolved—and which the lower mind had been utterly unable to comprehend. To act as the matured new consciousness of the giant Earth-life organism.

THE END

IT WAS NO ORDINARY HEADACHE...

It seemed like the worst headache imaginable. Pete Miller felt like his head was going to explode. But it turned out to be no ordinary headache. Pete's suspicions were aroused when the TV set at Art's bar went on the fritz. Then the engine in Freddie's new car blew up. The next victim was the jukebox across the street at the High Hat. Not much later, another jukebox, this one at Harry's place, also mysteriously broke down. But what could be causing all the trouble? Surely Pete's throbbing brain couldn't be culprit…

T. L. Sherred spins a very memorable tale of a man with a headache—who found a cure for it. And that cure gave him more power than any man could ever dream of…

ABOUT T. L. SHERRED:

Thomas L. Sherred was born in Detroit, Michigan on August 27th, 1915. He was the author of a small number of science fiction tales, consisting of a few stories, two short novels, a long novel, and the beginning of another novel that was completed by Lloyd Biggle, Jr. after Sherred's death. Although his output was small, Sherred's short novel, "E for Effort" (*Astounding Science Fiction,* May, 1947) was voted into the Science Fiction Hall of Fame.

Sherred's longest work, the novel "Alien Island," was published in 1970. "Alien Island" deals with the horrendous events that occur when extraterrestrials covertly inhabit Earth. His writing career came to a halt in 1971 after he suffered a stroke.

Soon after his death, Sherred's unfinished follow-up to "Alien Island," was finished by Lloyd Biggle, Jr., and published as "Alien Main." This sequel was set on Earth 200 years after nearly all life had been destroyed by aliens. The novel finds alien descendants coming to Earth to atone for the atrocities committed by their ancestors.

Thomas L. Sherred passed away on the sixteenth day of April, 1985.

CUE FOR QUIET

By
T. L. SHERRED

ARMCHAIR FICTION
PO Box 4369, Medford, Oregon   97501-0168

*For more information about Armchair Books and products, visit our
website at…*

www.armchairfiction.com

Or email us at…

armchairfiction@yahoo.com

PART ONE

So I had a headache. The grandfather of all headaches. You try working on the roof line sometime, with the presses grinding and the overhead cranes wailing and the mechanical

arms clacking and grabbing at your inner skull while you snap a shiny sheet of steel like an armored pillowcase and shove it into the maw of a hungry greasy ogre. Noise. Hammering, pounding, shrieking, gobbling, yammering, incessant noise. And I had a headache.

This headache had all the signs of permanency. It stayed with me when I slid my timecard into an empty slot that clanged back at me, when I skittered across a jammed street of blowing horns and impatient buses with brake drums worn to the rivets, when I got off at my corner and stood in the precarious safety of a painted island in a whirring storm of hurtling hornets. It got even worse when I ate dinner and tried to read my paper through the shrill juvenile squeals of the housing project where I live surrounded by muddy moppets and, apparently, faithless wives and quarrelsome spouses. The walls of my Quonset are no thicker than usual.

When Helen—that's my wife—dropped the casserole we got for a wedding present from her aunt and just stood there by the kitchen sink crying her eyes out in frustration I knew she finally had more of a mess to clean up than just the shattered remains of a brittle bowl. I didn't say a word. I couldn't. I shoved the chair across the room and watched it tilt the lamp her mother bought us. Before the lamp hit the floor my hat was on my head and I was out the door. Behind me I heard at least one pane of the storm door die in a fatal crash. I didn't look around to see if it were the one I'd put in last Sunday

ART WAS glad to see me. He had the beer drawn and was evening the foam before the heavy front door had shut us off from the street. "Been a while, Pete. What's new?"

I was glad to see him, too. It was quiet in there. That's why I go eight blocks out of my way for my beer. No noise, no loud talking or you end up on the curb; quiet. Quiet and dark and comfortable and you mind your own business, usually. "Got any more of those little boxes of aspirin?"

He had some aspirin and was sympathetic. "Headache again? Maybe you need a new pair of glasses."

I washed down the pills and asked for a refill on the beer. "Maybe, Art. What do you know that's new?"

Nothing. We both knew that. We talked for a while; nothing important, nothing more than the half-spoken, half-grunted short disjointed phrases we always repeated. Art would drift away and lean on the other end of the bar and then drift back to me and at the end of each trip there would be clean ashtrays and the dark plastic along the bar would gleam and there would be no dregs of dead drinks and the rows of fresh glasses would align themselves in empty rows on the stainless steel of the lower counter. Art's a good bartender when he wants to be. I held up my empty glass.

"One more, Art. Got the radio section of the paper?"

He handed it to me. "Might be something on the television."

We both laughed. We both feel the same way about television, but he has to have a set in his business for week-end football or baseball games. A big set he has, too, with an extra speaker for the far end of the bar for the short beer trade. I found the program I wanted and showed Art the listing.

He looked at it. "Strauss...that's that waltz music," and I nodded and he went over to the radio and found the station. These small stations can't sell every minute of their time for commercials, although they try, and every once in a while they run through a solid hour of Strauss or Bing Crosby or Benny Goodman. I like Strauss.

And there I sat drinking beer and eating stale popcorn when I should have been home with Helen, listening to quiet violins and muted brasses when I should have been doing something noisy and instructive. In my glass I could see whatever I wanted, wherever I would. I made circular patterns on the bar and drew them into a grotesque mass with fingers wet with the silver condensation of bubbles drawn magically through impervious crystal. Then Art turned off the radio.

He was apologetic, but he still turned off the radio. In answer to my unspoken question he shrugged and indicated Freddie. Freddie likes television. He likes dog acts and circus bands and bouncing clowns. He watches the commercials with an innocent unjaundiced eye. Sometimes he sings along with the animated bakers and cooks and gas stations at the top of his boyish beery baritone. He sings loud, and he likes his television the same way.

Art flipped up the lid of the television and stood there long enough to make sure the picture, whatever it was, would be in focus. Then he came back to me and poured another. Hesitating, he added another smaller glass. I can't afford that stuff on what I make. Where I made my mistake was taking it. We each had another. And another. The headache got worse.

Ivan and Jack came in, and, when they heard the blast of sound, came down to my end of the bar where, although the extra speaker is overhead, you don't have to look at the source of the noise. Art handed us a deck of cards and a piece of chalk to keep score and we started to play euchre. You don't have to think to play euchre, which is good. It's about the only game you can play with sign language, the only game for a noisy bar. So we played euchre, and at ten-thirty Ivan and Jack left me alone to face the music. The little cords at the nape of my neck were tight as wires, the temple areas near my eyes were soft and tender and sore to the touch, and my head was one big snare drum.

That was when Freddie half-shouted to Art to get the Roller Derby on Channel Seven and—so help me!—to turn it up a little louder. The cards fell out of my hand and onto the table. I took out a cigarette and my lighter slipped out of my tight fingers and fell on the floor and I bent over to pick it up. My head swelled to twice its size, my glasses slid down a little on my sweaty nose, and the tiny red veins in my eyes grew from a thread to a rope to a flag to a tapestry of crimson rage and the noise abruptly stopped. And Art began to bellow. I stood up. The television set was smoking.

Well, it was fast while it lasted. Art didn't really need the fire department. There wasn't any flame to speak of. Someone pulled the plug from the wall and rolled the set out and used the hand extinguisher on the burnt innards of the set and with the rear exhaust fan going the last of the bitter smoke was drifting out before the sirens pulled up in front. The firemen were relieved, not angry, as they always are, and Art in his misery was thoughtful enough to slip a square bottle in the pocket of the lieutenant in charge. It was cold outside, at that. Freddie said so, when he left; there was no reason to stay at Art's any more when most other bars would have the Roller Derby. I watched him go, and mentally cursed the bearings in his new car. Well, fairly new. I went home. Helen was in bed when I got there, probably asleep. She was still probably asleep when I left for work in the morning. She gets like that.

The next day at Art's there was a big space lighter in color than the surrounding wall where the television set had stood. I asked Art about it.

He didn't know. The serviceman had come out and collected it, clucking in dismay at the mess the extinguisher had left. No, no idea what caused it. Short circuit wouldn't make it that bad; fuses should have blown first. They'd find it, though. Art hoped it wouldn't be the picture tube; that wasn't covered in his service policy, and those tubes in that size cost money. Anything else was covered. At that, he was better off than Freddie.

I looked up. "What's the matter with Freddie?"

He told me. Freddie had ruined his motor on the way home last night. What hadn't blown out the exhaust pipe had gone out the hood, and right after his ninety-day guarantee had expired.

I remembered what I had thought of last night. "How did he do that?"

Art didn't know. He had been driving along and—that was it. The car was in the garage with nothing left between the radiator and the firewall and Freddie was trying to get something out of the insurance company. Fat chance, too, with that bunch of pirates. We'd all had experience with that sort of thing, hadn't we? Why—someone at the other end of the bar wanted some service and Art left. I sat back and began to add two and two. I got five.

Art came back and grinned at me. "You're not going to like this, Pete."

"What won't I like?"

"This," and a man in coveralls shouldered me aside and set a cobra on the bar in front of me, a snake with a twelve inch tube. Art went on to explain: "They're giving me a loaner until my own set gets back and they don't want to plug it in the usual place until they get a chance to completely check the wiring. Okay?"

It had to be okay. It wasn't my place of business. I moved down a bit and watched the serviceman plug it in. He tried the channels for clarity and without warning flipped the volume control all the way over and the whole building shook. I shook, too, like a bewildered Labrador throwing off an unwanted splash of icy water. The top of my head lifted from its moorings and shifted just enough for me to name that infernal serviceman and all his issue. He just sat there and grinned, making no attempt to tone down the set. Then I said what I thought about his television, and the set went quiet. Like that.

It began to smoke and the serviceman began to shuck tools from his box. Art opened his mouth to yell and I walked out the front door. The High Hat, right across the street, would serve to keep me warm until the smoke and profanity was cleared and Art had the repairman under control.

I knew it! They had a jukebox inside the door with the same twenty top tunes of the week, the same gaudy front with the same swirling lights and the same tonsillectomied tenors. I shuddered as I eased by, and I murmured a heartfelt wish over my shoulder, something about the best place for that machine. I ordered a beer, a short one. The barkeep, a pleasant enough fellow, but with none of Art's innate joviality, rang up the dime.

"You didn't happen to pull the cord out when you walked by, did you?"

"Pull the cord out of what?"

He didn't bother to answer, and went over to the machine. That was the first I realized the music had stilled. He clicked the switch on and off a few times with no result, and went to the telephone, detouring by way of the cash register to pick up a coin. Thoughtfully sipping my beer I heard him dial and report a jukebox out of order. Then a relay clicked in the back of my head.

Could all this be a coincidence? Could be... Couldn't be! The beer grew warm in my hand as I remembered. Every time I'd wished, really wished hard, something had happened. Now that I had time to think it over I remembered that red rotor spinning madly past my eyes, that horrible hatred and afterward, that sated sense of fulfillment... Better have another beer and forget it, Pete. Better make it two beers. Maybe three.

The High Hat sold me a lot more than two beers, or three. When I left there, although I was walking a mental chalk line I had a little trouble lighting a cigarette in the chill breeze. I didn't bother going back to Art's. Art was all right, and there was no sense in making trouble for a pal. Harry, now. He was a stinker. Go put the needle in Harry, two blocks away.

While Harry was drawing the beer I walked string straight to the jukebox, clicked in a quarter, and stalked back to the barstool. Turn your back, Pete, just as though you didn't know perfectly well what was going to happen. Now take a tasty sip of your beer, wait for the noise to start... Take a deep breath, now; Pete Miller, savior of man's sanity. I closed my eyes and pretended to be covering a yawn.

"Tubes," I whispered, "do your stuff. Blow that horn, Gabriel—go ahead and—blow!"

The jukebox moaned as far as the first eight bars; I got my quarter back from a puzzled Harry; I listened to Harry call his repairman; I finished my beer; I got outside and almost around the corner before I began laughing like a hyena; I got to bed snickering and went to sleep the same way; and I woke up with a headache.

Hammering presses the next day I treated with the contempt of long practice. One single theme kept rolling around like a pea in a washtub; just what had happened to that television set and those jukeboxes? And what had made a fairly new eight-cylinder almost disintegrate, apparently on command? Agreed, that coincidence has a mighty long arm, but hardly long enough to scratch its own elbow. Forty years old and a superman? One way to find out. Let's go at this cold sober. Let's scratch this shiny new rubber band until it snaps.

AT THREE-THIRTY I was first in line at the time clock, second out the gate, and fourth or fifth to line up at the National Bar. "Aspirin and ginger ale," I ordered, and got a knowing grin from the barkeep. Laugh, buddy. You may think I feel bad now, but wait and see what happens to your bangbox. I dare someone to put in a nickel; I double-dare you. That's it—pick a good number from one to twenty and go back to your stool and sit down. Take it easy, now, Pete. Don't strain, don't press, no slugging in the clinches, and break clean. The place needs a good airing, anyway, and the floor could use a new broom, too. Bubble, bubble, go for double...no more music. No more noise. Smoke, you boiler factory, smoke! Hey, somebody, pull that plug. Not that one, *that* one. Pull it out. Pull it out! *Pull it out!*

Finally someone did pull it out, someone chattered excitedly into the telephone, and I slid out the front door when the fire engines were wailing blocks away. Coincidence, hey. And cold sober, too. I stood on the curb and watched the firemen dash in and straggle out. Dirty trick to break up a pinochle game in weather like this. Four red-eyed crimson giants snorted and whined their blunt noses back into the clogged traffic, back to wait another call. Three buses were sentinels at the safety zone, and one of them took me home to dinner. This was on a Friday, the night for the Olsens, next door, to have their weekly Sanger bund. When Helen shook me into wakefulness the party was going strong.

"Pete, will you wake up? You know perfectly well when you hear me!"

Yes, I heard her. "What time is it?"

"Never mind what time it is. You go over there and tell them you're going to call the police if they don't turn off that radio—"

I yawned. "After two o'clock."

"Almost two-thirty. You just get up and—"

I laughed out loud, as loud as you can laugh at that time of the morning. "Roll over and go back to sleep," I told her. "They'll shut it off in a minute."

I shut my sleepy lids and went through the deep breath routine. The radio stopped. Then an afterthought; this was Friday, and I wanted to sleep late on a Saturday unsullied and unwelcomed by soap operas. Another deep breath, complicated by a yawn, and I went back to sleep.

OVER OUR coffee Helen pulled aside the kitchen curtain.

"I thought there was some reason I didn't wake up until ten. Look across the street," and she pointed.

In front of the Olsen's, a red panel truck, Chuck's Radio Service. Next door, in front of the Werner's, Harper Radio Parts. In the Smith's driveway, Rapid Radio Repair.

"What are you grinning at?"

"Me? I'm not grinning. Not at this time of the morning."

"Pete Miller, you were, too. Just like the cat that ate the fish."

"Canary, you mean."

"That's what I said. What's so funny?"

"Nothing," I said. "We just got a good night's sleep for a change. I like my sleep."

She *harrumphed* a bit, as suspicious as she usually is, and I went to the stove for more coffee. Over my shoulder I said, "Want to play a little cards tonight?"

She was skeptical about that. "At Art's, I suppose."

"Sure. Saturday night euchre tournaments."

"That noisy place? Nothing doing."

I told her the jukebox and the television set were out of commission and there'd be no noise she didn't make herself. She loved to play cards, I knew, and she liked Art. It was just the incessant roar that wore her down. I managed to talk her into it.

AT ART'S that night I listened with envy to the words that were used over the telephone when the jukebox gave up its ghost. I heard only Art's end of the conversation, of course, but I gathered that Art was being accused at the very least of blatant sabotage. I changed the subject quick when I caught Helen trying to figure out the look I must have been wearing. Women get so they're pretty good at that after they've been married awhile. Art himself drove us home at closing time. Helen and Art's wife did all the talking, and I'm sure no one noticed I held my breath before every bar or house and Helen commented, as I fit the key into the front door, on the fact that the Olsens and the Werners and the Smiths all picked the same time to turn off their radios. "Very nice of them," she said, "considering it's Saturday night."

Now, I use two buses to get to work, transferring from the Harper bus to the Clairmount line, and it's a forty minute ride. For two days I fed my ego by holding my breath. I likely looked queer with a bursting red face, but no one said anything, at least directly to me. I wouldn't have cared much, anyway, because I didn't care much what happened; after all, wasn't I a benefactor to practically all the human race, the thinking part, that is? Wasn't it going to be nice to live in a world without punctured eardrums and hamstrung nerves? Wasn't it going to be good to be able to eat a meal in peace, to sip your ten or sixty-cent drink without having some moron with a nickel prodding your ulcer? I thought so.

Thursday, or maybe Friday, my careful searching of the daily papers found my tiny item buried back of the stock reports, with the labor news. I read it three times.

JUKEBOX WAR SUSPECTED

An anonymous tip today told our labor reporter that serious trouble looms in the canned music industry. R. C. Jones, czar of Local 77, AFL, has issued orders to individually guard each machine serviced by his union. Jones had the classic "no comment" for publication, but it is an open secret that intra-union friction is high in the Harper-Gratiot area. Jones inferred that deliberate sabotage is responsible for the wholesale short-circuiting of jukeboxes and television sets. He named no names, but in an off-the-record statement threatened to fight fire with fire. "We're not," he snapped, "going to stand by and watch while goons ruin our livelihood. We will..."

Now I was in a fix. They had to make a living. I'd forgotten that. A union man myself, who was I to break another's rice bowl? I could see no point in writing to this R. C. Jones. He'd think I was as crazy as they come. And the newspapers—I could imagine the reactions of a tough city editor. So, wrapped up in my own thoughts, I stepped off the curb a little ahead of the green, and I jumped just in time. I swore at the truck that almost got me, and it happened so quickly I wasn't prepared to hear or to see the motor of the truck throw a piston right through the rusted hood. White as a sheet the driver got out of his cab, and I crossed the street against the red light and lost myself in the crowd. This curve I was putting on the ball, it came to me then, wasn't limited to jukeboxes and noisy radios and burnt-out bearings. I had to watch my temper, or I was going to get someone in trouble. I was in trouble myself, and I had to get out of it.

By the time I got home I'd thought it over quite well. This—this power whatever it might be, was the McCoy. Why should I waste it when an honest dollar might be turned? A factory job in Detroit is just a factory job, and I might keep mine for the next forty years if I lived long enough through the noise and the dirt and the uncertainty and the model changeover layoffs every Christmas. The Olsens' radio disturbed my thinking and it took only a second. Either they were going to get tired of putting new tubes into that gadget, or play it softer, or move. I didn't care which.

So I used my wife's portable to type out a letter to Naval Ordnance in Aberdeen where my brother-in-law used to be stationed, telling them what I'd done, what I thought I might be able to do, and asking them for an opportunity to give them a demonstration. In return, I asked for a steady government job in a warm climate. Until I could arrange a certain demonstration, I went on, I could understand they might think me a crank, so I wouldn't at present sign my name. I suggested they pay close attention through the week of the fifth through the twelfth to the various press association dispatches, and I would arrange later, in my next letter, for a more personal show if they wanted to take it any further.

THE FIFTH fell on a Saturday. Bright and early I was up to ride the bus downtown, changing to the Woodward line, ending up at Ferndale, all the time concentrating furiously and holding my breath as much as I dared. On the way back home I tried to work it a little differently. Probably no one else on the streetcar beside myself noticed there wasn't a single passenger car, truck or bus that passed us. Every car, as we sailed by, stalled and every traffic light we passed either turned three colors or blinked out completely. Most of the moving cars made it to the curb on their momentum. The others stayed where they were. When I got off in front of the City Hall, filthy old hulk that it is, the streetcar stayed immobile at the safety zone, it was a new P. C. C. car, and the insulation poured smoke from under the wheels. Naturally there wasn't any moving traffic in back of it, or in front. I saw to that. Then I just strolled around Cadillac Square, bollixing up everything that occurred to me, from trucks to busses to traffic lights. You never saw such a verminous tangled mess in all your life. When the patrol wagons began to scream into the Square loaded with reinforcements for the helpless purple single cop at the Michigan intersection I let them get as far as the center of the street before I pinned them down. Even when I saw it later in the newsreels I couldn't believe it. Even Mack Sennett could have done no better.

I had to walk all the way out Gratiot to St. Antoine before I could find transportation home that wasn't walled off by screaming horns and haggard foot-patrolmen, and when I got off at my corner all Gratiot and Harper behind me was as clogged as Woodward. I even knocked out every red neon sign within two blocks of a traffic light. That one might keep a few pedestrians alive a little longer.

Helen was over at her mother's helping her hang drapes when I got home. The icebox gave me a cold Jumbo bottle and I turned on our little portable set. On every station the spot broadcast crews were hoarse. I spun the dials and finally concentrated on one announcer—you know who I mean— with the raspiest, most grating voice this side of a vixen file. Unfortunately, the housewives seem to like him, including Helen, and it's the housewives who have the radio on all day. I knew he was broadcasting from the roof studios of one of our highest buildings, and I took an enormous and perverted pleasure in holding my breath and thinking about the elevator system there. On second thought, I held my breath again and the station left the air in the middle of a word. I hope he liked the walk downstairs.

The newspapers next day couldn't make things add, as was natural. They published silly interviews with all the top engineers in the city and a good many all over the world, including the Chairman of the Board of the company where I worked, and his answer was just as asinine as the rest. All in all, it had been a good show, and I put in another letter to Naval Ordnance. I knew I had gone much further than I had intended, and I suggested they get in touch with me, if they wanted, through the personal columns of one of the Detroit newspapers. I didn't want to get into trouble with the city police. I didn't sign my name to the second letter either. And that was a mistake.

EARLY IN the morning of the tenth I felt good. I'd been sleeping well lately, now that I was rid of the Olsens' radio, not to mention the Werners', and the Smiths'. I rolled over and squinted at the luminous hands of the' clock. Beer cheese in the icebox. Half a Dutch apple pie left over from dinner. Milk. Helen didn't wake as I eased out of bed and groped for my slippers, and the rustling and shuffling I heard as I tiptoed down the back stairs I attributed to an over-brave mouse. One of these days, I thought, I was going to have to get some traps and catch me a mouse. When I turned on the kitchen light the mouse was holding a howitzer nine inches away from my head.

"All right, you," the mouse snarled. "Reach!"

I reached. Quick.

The gunman backed to the outside door and flicked it open with one hand, never taking his eyes from me. Footsteps pounded on the back porch and hard faces filled the kitchen. One even had one of these gas-pipe Sten guns, and I liked that even less than the howitzer. My pajama tops might have concealed an arsenal from the care I got when I was searched. No one said a word, and I didn't dare. Just about that time Helen got the sandman out of her eyes. Likely the noise had awakened her appetite, and she had come down to help me eat a snack. One of the gunmen heard her slippers clattering down the stairs, and a hard hand slapped over my mouth and a gun rammed viciously against my spine. Spun around and held as a human shield I had to helplessly watch her come yawning in the kitchen door. She got one look in at me and the drawn guns. Then her mouth opened to scream but got no further than a muffled yip and a

dead faint. They let her fall. The gunman took his hand from my mouth and swung me around.

"Shut up!" he snapped, although I hadn't tried to say anything.

At the point of his gun he held me there while the rest of the hard faced crew roamed the house, upstairs and down. None of the faces did I know, and I began to wonder if behind one of those granite masks was the revengeful personality of R. C. Jones, President of Local 77, A. F. L. I heard footsteps pad on the back porch, and my head tried to turn in spite of myself. The gun in my back gouged a little harder. Out of the corner of my eye I could see who pushed open the screen door I hadn't got around to taking down yet. The gun in my back helped me stand up.

J. Edgar Hoover motioned to the gun and the pressure eased a trifle. His voice was reasonably unexcited, but to my present taste, ominous.

"All right. Someone go get him some pants." To me, "Your name Miller? Peter Ambrose Miller? Get that woman off the floor."

Yes, I was Peter Ambrose Miller. I agreed to that. My mouth was dry as popcorn, but I managed to ask him what this was all about.

Hoover looked at me and scratched his nose. "This is about your fingerprints being all over an anonymous letter received in Aberdeen, Maryland."

I gulped. "Oh, that. Why, I can explain—"

Hoover looked at me with the fond expression of a man who has cracked open a bad egg. "That," he said, "I doubt," and he turned on his military heel and walked out the back door. When they got me my pants I followed him. I had to.

I ended up at the Federal Building, which is a cavernous morgue, even during business hours. They gave me what might have been a comfortable chair if I hadn't had to sit in it. A young fellow was sitting opposite me with a stenographer's notebook, and I knew that any story of mine had better not be repeated two different ways. Hoover came in with a nondescript man with a hat pulled down over his eyes, who inspected me from all angles and then shook his head, a little resentfully, I thought. The hat-over-the-eyes left and I shifted nervously under those grim eyes staring at me.

"All right," said Hoover; "now we'll hear that explanation. Talk!"

So I talked.

When I finished my throat was dry and he was nodding as though he believed every word. He didn't. I asked for a cigarette and for news of my wife, and they gave me a cigarette. They told me my wife was all right, or would be, if I behaved.

"Don't worry," I said. "I'll behave." They just laughed when I said that.

"Quite likely," said Hoover. "Now, let's hear that once more. Begin at the beginning."

They gave me a room all to myself, finally. For three days, maybe more, I had that room all for myself and the various people that walked in at all hours of the day and night to ask me some of the silliest questions you ever heard just as though they expected sensible answers. After that first night I didn't see J. Edgar Hoover at all, which is just as well, because I don't think he liked me one little bit. They brought me a suit with the lining in the sleeve ripped and a shirt with the cuffs turned. When I got those I began to worry all over again about Helen, because I knew she had no part in picking out the clothes they brought me. I didn't feel too chipper when they came after me in force again.

The same room, this time more crowded. Older men this time, and a few of the usual high school boys. Again we went through the same routine, and once again my voice cracked dusty dry. They were all desperately sorry for such an incurable psychopathic liar. I hadn't felt so helpless, so caught-in-a-quicksand since my days in the army.

"I'm telling you the truth, the truth. Don't you see that I've got to tell you the truth to get out of here? Don't you believe me?"

Never such disbelief outside of a court-martial. In desperation my eyes jerked around looking for escape. They slid over, and back to, the ventilation fan purring on the wall. I sucked in a loud gasp. The blades of the fan slowed to where you could see them as individuals, and the motor housing began to smoke.

"See?" I yelled at them. "Believe me now?"

The blades came to a standstill and the black smoke oozed toward the ceiling.

"See?" I yelled again. "Look at that fan!"

Their eyes showed their astonishment. The smoke began to disappear in the stillness. "What about that? Now do you believe me?"

Maybe they did. No one said anything. They took me back to my room. About an hour or so later they came after me again. The chair felt no more comfortable than it ever had, though it was beginning to shape itself to my seat. The same faces were there, but the air was a little different this time. On the desk, where I had seen sit no one but J. Edgar Hoover were a half dozen fans, plugged to an extension cord that snaked away and lost itself in a dark corner. My ears twitched hopefully. Maybe this was going to get me out of here. One of the younger men spoke up.

"Mr. Miller," he said briskly, "can you stop these fans as you did, apparently, the other?"

I started to tell him that "apparently" wasn't the right word. One of the older men broke in.

"One moment," he said. "Can you stop any one of these fans, or all of them? Any particular one, and leave the rest alone?"

I thought I could. "Which one?" There were five fans whirring silently away.

"Well...the one in the center."

The one in the center. One out of five. Hold your breath, Peter Ambrose, hold it now or you can hold your breath the rest of your natural life and no one will ever know, nor ever care. The fan in the center began to smoke and the blades choked off abruptly.

I said, "The one on the far left...the one next to it...the far right...and four makes five." I watched the last blade make its last swing. "Has anybody got a cigarette?"

I got a full package. While I tore off the cellophane someone held a light. I filled my lungs so full they creaked and sat back defiantly.

"So now what?"

No one knew just what. Two men slipped out and the others drew together their chairs for a whispered conference full of dark looks in my direction. I sat quietly and smoked until even that got on my nerves. Finally I broke it up with a yell.

"Can't you fatheads make up your minds? Don't you know what you want? Do you think I'm going to sit here all night?"

That was a stupid question; I knew I was going to sit there until they told me to get up. But at the time I wanted to say it, and I did, and I said other things that were neither polite nor sensible. I was a little upset, I think. It didn't matter. They paid no attention to me, so I lit another cigarette and waited. The outer door opened and one of the two that had left came back in. He came directly to me, waving the others out as he came. They filed out and he stood in front of me.

"Mr. Miller. This is rather an awkward situation for all of us, particularly for you, obviously. I want to say this, Mr. Miller; I—that is, we here in the Bureau are extremely sorry for the turn of events that brought both of us here. We—"

At the first decent word I'd heard in days I blew up. "Sorry? What's being sorry going to do for me? What's being sorry going to do for my wife? Where is she? What's happened to her? Where is she, and what are you doing to her? And when am I going to get out of here?"

He was a polite old man, come to think about it. He let me blow off all the steam I'd been saving, let me rant and rage, and clucked and nodded in just the right places. At last I ran down, and he moved a chair to where he could be confidential. He started like this:

"Mr. Miller, I, speaking personally, know exactly how you must feel. Close custody is as unpleasant for the jailor as it is for the one in jail, if there is such a word, sir."

I snorted at that one. A jail is a jail, and the turnkey can walk out if he chooses.

"You must remember that you are and have been dealing with an official agency of the Government of the United States of America, of which you are a citizen; an agency that, officially or otherwise, can never be too careful of any factor that affects, however remotely, the security or safety of that Government. You understand that quite well, don't you, Mr. Miller?" He didn't wait to find out if I did. "For that reason, and for no other, you were brought here with the utmost speed and secrecy, and kept here."

"Oh, sure," I said. "I'm going to blow up a tax collector, or something like that."

He nodded. "You might."

"Blah. So you made a mistake. So you're sorry, so my wife is probably completely out of her head by now, I'm crazy myself, and you want to talk politics. All I want to know is this—when do I get out of here?"

He looked at me with an odd, queer smile. "This, Mr. Miller, is where the shock lies. I think, diametrically opposite to the opinions and, I might add, to the direct pleadings of some of my colleagues involved in this rather inexplicable affair, that you are the adaptable Teutonic type that likes to know exactly the odds against him, the type of man who likes to know where and when he stands."

"I know exactly where I stand," I told him. "I want to know just one thing; when do I get out of this rat trap?"

He mulled that over, his forehead wrinkled as he searched for the right words. "I'm afraid, Mr. Miller, very much afraid that you're going to get out of here very soon. But never out of any place else." And with that he walked out the door before I could lift a finger to stop him.

But when they came after me to put me away I wasn't stunned. It took four of them, and one more that came in as reinforcement. They weren't rough deliberately, but they weren't easy. They had a time, too. I think I've been around long enough to know a few dirty tricks. I used them all, but I still went back to my room, or cell. I got no sleep at all for the rest of the night, nor most of the next night. I wondered if I could ever sleep again. If someone had mentioned "Helen" to me I likely would cry like a baby. I couldn't get her out of my mind.

When they came after me again they were all prepared for another argument. I didn't care, this time. Meekly I went along, back to that same conference room. Four men; the old man who had given me the spurs before, one of the high school boys, and a couple of uniforms. The old man stood up very formally to greet me.

"Good morning, Mr. Miller."

I snarled at him. "Good for what?"

One of the uniforms was indignant. "Here, here, my man!"

I let him have it, too. "In your hat, fatty. My discharge went on the books in forty-five!" He was shocked stiff, but he shut up.

The old man kept his face straight. "Won't you sit down, Mr. Miller?" I sat. I still didn't like the chair. "This is General Hayes, and this is General Van Dorf." They nodded stiffly, and I ignored them. He didn't introduce the young man, not that I cared.

"Mr. Miller, we'd like to talk to you. Talk seriously."

"Afraid that I'll get mad and fly out the window?"

"I said seriously. It won't take long. Let's compress it into one short sentence without the preliminaries: give these gentlemen a demonstration like the last one."

I told him what he could do with his demonstration, and I told him what he could do with his generals. The high school boy grinned when I said that. He must have been old enough to have served in the army.

The generals were crimson. You don't get that kind of talk where they worked. But the old man was unperturbed. "Let's make that one sentence a paragraph. Give these gentlemen a demonstration as effective as the last—and ten minutes after, if you like, you can walk out of here free as the air."

I jumped at that. "Is that straight? If I do it again you'll let me loose?"

He nodded. "If you really want to."

I persisted. "Straight, now? On your word of honor?"

He wasn't lying. "If you want my word you have it."

I grinned all over like a dog. "Bring on your fans, or whatever you have cooked up."

The young man went out and came right back in with a little cartload of electric fans. Either they had too many for general use, or someone had very little imagination. Come summer, with Detroit ninety in the shade, they were going to miss their ventilation. Me, I was going to be a long way from the Federal Building. He set the fans on the desk, and the generals craned stork-like to see what was going on. The old man bowed to them.

"Name one, gentlemen. Any one you like." They named the middle one again.

I CALLED my shots again, as free and easy as though I'd been doing it for years. "The middle one first, you say? No sooner said than done, gentlemen. Right? Right! Now the far left, and right down the line. Eeney, meeny, and out goes me." They were all dead, and I stood up and asked the room, "Which is the express elevator to the main floor?"

The old man held up his hand. "One moment, Mr. Miller." He read my mind, which, at that second, wasn't hard to do. "Oh, no. You're free to go any time you so desire. But I would like to make this demonstration a little more convincing."

He meant it. I could go if I liked.

"You also, Mr. Miller, as I understand it, exhibit somewhat the same degree of control over internal combustion engines." And well he knew I did. That traffic tie-up I'd engineered had traveled via newsreels all over the world. "Will you gentlemen step over to the window?" This was to me and the generals.

We all crowded over. I looked down and saw we were on the ninth floor, maybe the eighth or tenth. It's hard to judge distance when you're looking straight down.

"Mr. Miller—"

"Yeah?"

"If one of these officers will pick out a car or a truck down on the street below can you stop it? Stop it dead in its tracks?"

"Sure. Why not?"

"All right, then. General Hayes, we'll let you do the honors. Will you select from all those cars down there any particular item?"

I broke in. "Or any streetcar." I was feeling cocky.

"Or any streetcar. I would suggest, General, that you choose a target for its visibility. One that you cannot mistake."

The uniforms were suspicious, as they conferred with their noses flat against the glass. They beckoned to me and pointed.

"That one there."

"Which one where?" They had to be more explicit than that.

"The big truck. The one with the green top and the pipe sticking out."

I spotted it. It slowed for a red light, and came to a complete stop. I concentrated. Blow, Gabriel.

The cross traffic halted, and the truck again got under way. Then suddenly, as it must have been, although from where we were it seemed like a leisurely stroll, it veered through the other traffic lane and smoke burst from its hood. We could see the driver pop from his seat and race to the corner fire alarm box. Almost instantly traffic both ways was four deep. I turned away from the window. I don't like heights, anyway.

"Now can I go?" Walk, not run to the nearest exit.

The old man spoke directly to the uniforms, "Well, gentlemen, are you satisfied?"

They were satisfied, all right. They were stunned. They were probably visualizing a stalled tank retriever, a stalled 6x6.

"Thank you, Mr. Miller. Thank you very much." My grin was wide, as I started for the door.

"But I think that it is only fair, before you go, for me to tell you one thing."

With my hand on the knob, I laughed at him. "You mean that there isn't any Santa Claus?"

The corners of his mouth went up. "Not for you, I'm afraid. Are you insured?"

"Me? Insured? You mean the extra thirty cents I give the newsboy every week?"

"That's it. Insured. Life insurance."

I shrugged. "Sure. A couple of thousand as long as I take the papers."

"Suppose your subscription expires, or is cancelled, for certain reasons that should be obvious?" The generals stopped fidgeting and looked curiously at the old man.

I couldn't figure out what he meant, and said so.

"You can—well, let's say that you can 'interfere' with electrical or mechanical devices, can't you?"

Sure I could. At least, all the ones I'd ever tried.

"So, with that established, you would be in a military sense the theoretically perfect defense."

I hadn't thought about it that way. But if it ever came down to it I should be able to knock down an airplane, gum up the works on a fusing detonator, maybe even—. No, I didn't like that idea. Not me. Not at all.

The old man's voice was hard and soft at the same time. "So you're the irresistible force, or maybe the immovable object. And if you walk out of this office right now—and you can, Mr. Miller, that was our agreement—knowing what you know and being able to do what you have been doing... Now, just how long do you think it would take the intelligence of a dozen different nations to catch up with you? And how long after that would you stay 'free,' as you put it?

134

Or how long would you stay alive? There are all types of ways and means, you know." You bet I knew that.

My hair tried to stand on end. "Why, you'd be just cutting your own throat! You'd have to keep an eye on me. You can't back out on me now!"

He was sympathetic. "That's just what we're trying to do. We're trying to protect you and all you want to do is go home."

I sat down in the old chair. "So that's why you said I could go any time I wanted to." The old man said nothing. I ran my hands through my hair and tried to find the right words. "Now what?"

One of the generals started a preparatory cough, but the old man beat him to it. "I have a suggestion, Mr. Miller. You likely will not approve. Or, then again, you might."

"Yeah?"

"You know by now that this room, or its rough equivalent, is where you can be safe. This place, or one as well guarded."

"Yeah. And then what?"

He tried to make it as easy as he could. "Voluntarily—remember that word, and what it means—voluntarily put yourself in our charge. Put yourself under our care and our protection—"

"And your orders!"

General Van Dorf couldn't hold in his snort. "Good Heavens, man, where's your patriotism? Where's your—"

He got the worst of that exchange, and he didn't like it. "Where's your brains, man? Whatever patriotism I have left is pretty well worn after thirty-two months overseas. I'm sick of the Army and Navy; I'm sick of hurrying up to stand in line; I'm sick of being told what to do, and being told how and where to do it; I'm sick of being bossed. As far as I'm concerned there's only one person in this world who can tell me to do anything—and what's happened to my wife, anyway? Where is she? And where does she think I am right now?" The old man hesitated. "She doesn't know where you are. She's in the woman's division, downstairs. She's been well-treated, of course—"

"Sure. Well-treated." That was when I got really mad. "Sure. Jerk her out of bed in the middle of the night and throw her in jail and give her enough to eat and a place to sleep and that's supposed to be good treatment!"

The generals left without excusing themselves. Evidently they knew what was coming and wanted no part of it. The old Army game of signing your name and letting the sergeant hear the howls. I think that was the only thing that kept me there, as furious as I was, to hear what the old man had to say. He had been handed the dirty end of the stick, and he had to get rid of it the best way he could. When they were gone he circled a bit and then got the range.

BOILED DOWN, it was like this. "As of right now, you no longer exist. There is no more Peter Ambrose Miller, and maybe there never was. This I would suggest; your wife, being human, could keep quiet no longer than any other woman—or man. As far as she is concerned you're no longer alive. You were killed while escaping arrest."

The sheer brutality, the plain cruelty of that, almost drove me insane right there on the spot. I don't know what kept my hands off him. Now, of course, I realize that he was doing that deliberately to focus my hate on him, to present the bad side of it, to show me what could be done if I didn't cooperate. But I didn't know that then.

"So if I've got the name I'll have the game! Does it make any difference if I get shot in report or in fact? How would *your* wife like to know that you'd been shot down like a criminal? What would Helen say to her friends and my friends and her relatives and all the people we know?"

That was just the reaction he'd been waiting for. "I mentioned that only as a suggestion. That could be easily arranged another way. Let's say, for example, that you've been working for the Government ever since your legal discharge, in an undercover assignment, and you died in line of duty. It should be quite easy to see that your widow was awarded some sort of posthumous decoration. Would that help?"

I never thought that I would ever sit quietly and listen to someone calmly plot the complete obliteration of my whole life, my whole being. It was like one of these European novels when one sane man tries to live and find another sane person in a world of madness. A posthumous decoration. A medal for one that is dead and rotting. A nightmare with no waking up.

"And perhaps—oh, certainly!—a pension. You can rest assured your wife will never want. You see, Mr. Miller, we want to test you, and your...ability. Perhaps this unbelievable control you have can be duplicated, or understood. That we want to find out. We want to turn inside out all the enormous potential you have. In short we want—we must— have you in strictest custody and under rigid observation. If you like, I can see that you have a military or naval commission of rank commensurate with your importance. And don't think, Mr. Miller, that you're any less important than I've stated. Right now, from this side of the fence, it looks to me that you're the most important thing this side of the invention of the wheel."

I didn't want a commission. I wanted to lead a normal life, and I wanted my wife.

"The Marines, perhaps? Or the Air Corps?"

It wasn't just the Army, or the Navy; it was the system. If I had to be a Sad Sack I'd be a civilian.

"As you like. Agreed?"

I looked at him. "Agreed? What do you want me to say? Agreed. That's a good word for you to use to me."

"You can rest assured—" He saw what must have been on my face, and stopped short. For a long minute we sat there, he thinking his thoughts, and me thinking mine. Mine weren't pleasant. Then he got up and came over to me. "Sorry. This is a pretty big meal to digest all at once. I know how you must feel."

I stared up at him. "Do you?"

Then he turned and left. Later, I don't know when, the young fellow came back alone and took me to my cell. I must have finally gotten to sleep.

The young fellow, who turned out to be a fairly good citizen named Stein, came after me the next day. He wanted me to pack. Pack? All the clothes I had were on my back.

"Toothbrush, things like that. Tell me what you want in the line of clothes and you'll get them. Or anything else, within reason."

"Anything? Anything at all?"

"Well, I said anything reasonable." We didn't have to go any further into that. He knew what I meant.

When it was dark they took us away, Stein and myself. In the back of a mail truck, cramped and silent we rode for what seemed hours. Long before we rattled to a halt I could hear the familiar roars of motors being warmed. The tailgates swung open and a twenty-foot walk put us into a military ship. That meant Selfridge Field. Stein and I sat in the old painful bucket seats, the twin motors blasted and we trundled down the paved strip, a takeoff to nowhere. So long, Miller; so long to your wife and your home and your life. So long, Miller; you're dead and you're gone, and your wife will get a medal.

WHEN I AWOKE, the cabin was stuffy, and the sun was brassy and hot and high. Stein, already awake, came up with a thermos of coffee and a snack. A peep from the ports didn't tell me where I was, not that it mattered. Somewhere in the west or southwest, on a sandy waste on the far end of a landing strip away from a cluttered group of shacks, we walked long enough to get out the kinks. Then a hurried sandwich from a picnic basket left in the cabin by an invisible steward, and we transferred to a gray amphibian. The next time I had interest enough to look out and down we were over water, and toward the rim of the world we floated for hours. I dozed off again.

Stein woke me up. Wordlessly he passed me a heavy helmet, and the kind of goggles that present a mirrored blankness to the outside world. All this time I had seen none of the crews, even when we had landed. The two of us had strolled alone in a tiny world of our own. When the pilot cut his engines for the landing I had the old style helmet on my head. It was far too big, and hurt my ears. The galloping splash we made puddled the ports high, and we bobbed awkwardly until Stein got his signal from the pilot, who popped out an impersonal arm. From the wing-struts we transferred to a Navy dory, manned by enlisted men commanded by a blank-faced ensign in dungarees. We were both wearing the concealing helmets in the stifling heat, and the ensign's "Eyes Front," did no more than keep the sailors from sneaking curious looks from the corners of their eyes.

The small boat put us alongside what looked like more of a work ship than a fighter. It might have been an oiler or a repair-ship, or it might not have even been Navy. But it was Navy clean, and the crew was Navy. Some gold braid, way out of proportion to the size of the ship, met us at the top of the ladder, saluted, God knows why, and led Stein and I to a cabin. Not too big, not too small. I heard the amphibian rev up and take off again, and the deck tilted a trifle beneath us as we gathered way. A yank, and the suffocating helmet was off and I turned to Stein.

"Navy ship?"

He hesitated, then nodded.

"Navy ship."

"No beer, then."

I drew a big grin this time. He was human, all right. "No beer."

Like an oven it was in that cabin. In a shower stall big enough for a midget I splashed away until I got a mouthful of water. Salt. I paddled out of there in a hurry and spent the next two hours trying to get interested in a year-old House and Home. Hours? I spent three solid days looking at that same issue, and others like it. All the sailors on the ship must have had hydroponics or its equivalent on the brain. In between times it cost me thirteen dollars I didn't have to play gin with Stein. Then—

I NEVER did find out his real name. Neither his name, nor his job, nor what his job had to do with me, but he must have been important, from the salutes and attention he got. Maybe he'd just gotten there, maybe he'd been there all the time. He told me, when I bluntly asked him his name and what he did, that his name was Smith, and I still think of him as Smith. When he tapped on the door and stepped into that airless cabin I could smell the fans and the generals and the Federal Building all over again.

"Hello, Mr. Miller," he smiled. "Nice trip?"

"Swell trip," I told him. "Join the Navy and see the world through a piece of plywood nailed over a porthole."

When he sat down on the edge of the chair he was fussy about the crease in his pants. "Mr. Miller, whenever you are above decks, day or night, you will please keep your face concealed with that helmet, or its equivalent, no matter how uncomfortable the weather. Please."

"Since when have I been above decks? Since when have I been out of this two-by-four shack?"

"The shack," he said, "could be smaller, and the weather could be hotter. We'll see that while you're aboard you'll have the freedom of the deck after sunset. And you won't if things go right, be aboard much longer."

My ears went up at that. "No?"

"On the deck, upstairs..." He was no Navy man, or maybe that was the impression he wanted to give. "...are racks of rockets of various sizes. You might have noticed them when you came aboard. No? Well, they have been armed; some with electrical proximity fuses, some with mechanical timing devices, and some have both. They will be sent singly, or in pairs, or in salvos, at a target some little distance away. Your job will be the obvious one. Do you think you can do it?"

"Suppose I don't?"

He stood up. "Then that's what we want to know. Ready?"

I stretched. "As ready as I'll ever be. Let's go and take the air."

"Forget something?" He pointed at the helmet, hanging back of the door.

I didn't like it, but I put it on, and he took me up, up to the rocket racks on the prow. Even through the dark lenses the sun was oddly bright. Smith pointed off to port, where a battered old hull without even a deckhouse or a mast hobbled painfully in the trough of the sea.

"Target."

He jerked a thumb at the racks.

"Rockets."

I knew what they were. I'd seen enough of them sail over my head.

"Ready?"

Yes, I was ready. He made a careless flick of his hand and an order was barked behind me. A clatter and a *swoosh,* and a cylinder arced gracefully, catching me almost by surprise. I felt that familiar tightening behind my eyes, that familiar tensing and hunching of my shoulders. The propellant was taking the rocket almost out of sight when the fuse fired it. "Wham!"

Caught that one in midair. Try another. Another "whoosh," and another "wham."

Then they tried it in pairs. Both of the flying darning-needles blew together, in an eccentric sweep of flame. Four, maybe five or six pairs I knocked down short of the target, some so close to us that I imagined I could feel the concussion. They switched to salvos of a dozen at a time and they blew almost in unison. They emptied the racks that way, and I was grimly amused at the queer expression of the officer in charge as the enlisted men refilled the maws of the gaping racks. Smith, the old man, nudged me a little harder than necessary.

"All racks, salvo."

All at once. I tried for a cool breath in that sweaty helmet. "Ready!"

I couldn't pick out any individual sounds. The racks vomited lightning and thunder far too fast for that. The rumble and roar bored itself into a remote corner of my brain while I watched that barnacled hulk and concentrated. I couldn't attempt to think of each rocket, or each shot, individually, so I was forced to try to erect a mental wall and say to myself, "Nothing gets past that line *there*."

And nothing did. Just like slamming into a stone wall, every rocket blew up its thrumming roar far short of the target. The racks finally pumped themselves dry, and through the smoke Smith grasped my arm tighter than I liked. I couldn't hear what he was saying, deafened as we all were by the blasts. He steered me back to the cabin and I flipped off drops of sweat with the helmet. I turned unexpectedly and caught the old man staring at me.

"Now what's the matter with you?"

He shook his head and sat down heavily. "You know, Miller, or Pete, if you don't mind, I still don't actually believe what I've just seen."

I borrowed a light from the ubiquitous Stein. His expression told me he'd seen the matinee.

"I don't believe it either, and I'm the one that put on the show." I blew smoke in the air and gave back the lighter. "But that's neither here nor there. When do I get out of this Black Hole of Calcutta?"

"Well..." Smith was undecided. "Where would you like to spend some time when we're through with all this?"

That I hadn't expected. "You mean I have a choice?"

Noncommittally, "Up to a point. How about some island somewhere? Or in the States? Cold or warm? How, for instance, would you feel about Guam or—"

"Watched by the whole Mounted Police?" He nodded.

I didn't care. "Just someplace where no one will bother me; some place where I can play some records of the Boston Pops or Victor Herbert;" (and I guess the nervous strain of all that mental effort in all the noise and smoke was fighting a delaying action) "someplace where I can get all the beer I want, because it looks like I'm going to need plenty. Someplace where I can sit around and take things easy and have someone to—" I cut it short.

He was one of the understanding Smiths, at that. "Yes," he nodded, "we can probably arrange that, too. It may not be…" What else could he say, or what other way was there to say it?

"One more thing," he went on; "one more…demonstration. This will take some little time to prepare." That, to me, meant one thing, and I liked it not at all. He beat me to the punch.

"This should be what is called the pay-off, the final edition. Come through on this one, and you'll be better off than the gold in Fort Knox. Anything you want, anything that money or goodwill can buy, anything within the resources of a great—and, I assure you, a grateful—nation. Everything—"

"—everything," I finished for him, "except the right to go down to the corner store for a magazine. Everything except what better than me have called the pursuit of happiness."

He knew that was true. "But which is more important; your happiness, or the freedom and happiness of a hundred and seventy millions? Peter, if things political don't change, perhaps the freedom and happiness of over two billion, which, I believe, is the population of this backward planet."

"Yeah." The cigarette was dry, and I stubbed it in an ashtray. "And all this hangs on one person—me. That's your story." My mouth was dry, too.

His smile, I'm afraid, was more than just a little forced. "That's my story, and we're all stuck with it; you, me, all of us. No, you stay here, Stein. Let's see if we can get this over once and for all." Lines came and went on his forehead, as he felt for words.

"Let's try it this way: for the first time in written history as we know it one single deadly new weapon can change the course of the world, perhaps even change the physical course of that world, and the people who in the future will live in it. Speaking personally, as a man and as a reasonable facsimile of a technician, I find it extremely hard, almost impossible, to believe that at the exact psychic moment an apparent complete nullification of that weapon has appeared."

I grunted. "Maybe."

"Maybe. That's what we want to find out. Could you, Peter, if you were in my place, or you in your own place, get a good night's sleep tonight or any other night knowing that problem might have an answer without doing anything about it? Or are you one of these people who believe that there is no problem, that all things will solve themselves? Do you believe that, Stein? Do you think that Peter Ambrose Miller thinks that way?"

No, Stein didn't think that way, and Miller didn't think that way. We all knew that.

"All right," and he rubbed the back of his neck with a tired hand. "We have that weapon now. We, meaning the United States, and the whole wide world, from Andorra to Zanzibar. Now means today, in my lexicon. Tomorrow, and I mean tomorrow, or tomorrow of next year or the year after that, who will be the one to use that weapon? Do you know, Peter? Do you know?"

There was no need for an answer to that.

"And neither does anyone else. Peter, you're insurance. You're the cheapest and best insurance I know of. If! There's that big if. I hate that word. I always have, and I'm going to eliminate 'if,' as far as Peter Ambrose Miller is concerned. Right?"

Of course he was right. Hiroshima could just as well have been Memphis or Moscow or Middletown. And I always had wanted to be rich enough to carry my own insurance...

Before Smith left he told me it might be a month or two before he would see me again.

"These things aren't arranged overnight, you know."

I knew that.

I would be landed, he said, somewhere, someplace, and I'd be my own boss, up to a point. Stein would be with me, and the secrecy routine would still be in effect... His voice trailed off, and I neither saw nor heard him leave.

THREE MISERABLE weeks I spent somewhere in some stinking Southern Pacific mud hole. Cocker spaniel Stein was never out of reach, or sight, and gave me the little attention I wanted. From a distance I occasionally saw Army and Navy. The enlisted men were the ones who brought me not everything I asked for, but enough to get along. Later on, I knew, I'd get the moon on ice if I were actually as valuable as appeared. At that time no one was sure, including some brass who came poking around when they thought I might be asleep. They stayed far away from me, evidently under strict orders to do just that, although they took Stein aside several times and barked importantly at him. I don't think they made much impression on Stein. I was aching for an argument at that stage, and it's just as well they dodged contact. When Smith showed up, with the usual officious body-guard, I was itching to go.

Bikini I'd seen in the newsreels, and this wasn't it. The back forty would have dwarfed it. Just a limp palm or two and an occasional skinny lump of vegetation. Ships of all naval types and a civilian freighter or so spotted themselves at anchor like jagged rocks around the compass. The gray cruiser we were on never once dropped its hook; it paced nervously back and forth, up and down, and I followed, pacing the deck. With Stein at my heels, I saw daylight only through the ports. Only at night did I get to where I could smell the salt breeze free of the stink of paint and Diesel oil. From what I know about ships and their complements we must have had at least the captain's cabin, or pretty close to its mate. We never saw the captain, or at least he was never around when I was. The buzzing mass of brass and high civilians I knew were there, the old man told me, were and berthed on the big flattop carrier that idled off to port. Only Smith dropped in occasionally to rasp my frayed nerves deeper. With all the activity seething around us, and with only Stein and myself to keep each other company, we were getting cabin fever. I told that to Smith, who soothed me with promises.

"Tomorrow's the day."

"It better be. How are we going to work this, anyway?" I was curious, and I thought I had a right to be. "From what I hear, you better have your holes already dug."

"Too true," he agreed. "The bomb itself will be released from a drone plane, radio-controlled. We will, of course, be far enough from this island and the target installations you might have noticed going up to be out of range of radiations—"

"You hope!"

"—we hope. Your job will be to keep the bomb from detonating, or if that cannot be done, to fire it harmlessly, or as much so as possible. *That's* what we want to know. Clear?" Of course it was clear. That's what I wanted to know, too.

THE SUN came up out of the sea as quickly as it always does, and although the cruiser deck was almost bare far off we could see the carrier deck swarming with tiny ants. The odd-angled posts and gadgets we could see sticking up must have belonged to the technical boys, and they must have had plenty of it, if we could see it at that distance. Overhead they must have had at least eight planes of all types, from B-36's to helicopters to Piper Cubs, all dipping and floating and racing madly from one air bubble to another. Smith took time to tell me that, regardless whether the Bomb was fired by Miller or Iron Mike the explosion data would be immensely valuable.

"These things cost money," he said, "and this is killing two birds with one stone." I didn't want to be a bird, and my smile was sickly strained. Smith went off with a wry grin.

The helmet made the back of my neck itch and the glasses dug into the bridge of my nose. From the open space I had to work in they must have thought I was a ferry-boat, until it dawned on me that all those armed Marines with their backs turned weren't there just for ornament. Peter Valuable Miller. Very, very, queer, I thought, that all those technicians swarming on the carrier deck could be trusted enough to build and fire a Bomb and yet couldn't be allowed to know that there might be a possible defense to that Bomb. I watched Stein scratch his back against a projecting steel rib as the Smith strolled absently out of nowhere. Stein straightened sheepishly, and the old man smiled.

"Ready?"

Why not? I gave him the same answer as before. "Ready as I ever will be."

He handed me a pair of glasses, 7 x 50. "The drone ship took off ten minutes ago. Look due north—no, north is that way—and whenever it comes into whatever you consider your range—"

"Bingo!"

"Bingo!" He liked that. "When you fire it—"

"You mean, *if* I fire it."

"If you fire it, just before, you slide the filters over the ends of your binoculars like so. Or better still, turn your back."

Turn my back? I wanted to see what was going to happen.

"All right, but make sure you get those filters down in time." He cocked an ear as someone shouted something that was carried away in the freshening breeze. "Must have picked it up with radar. Let's see if we can find it," and together we set to sweeping the northern horizon.

Radar must have been sharp that day, because the drone, a battered B-24, was right on top of us before we picked it up, a mote in the sun's brazen eye. A flurry of orders relayed to the control ship sent it soaring back into the distance, a mile or so high. Just at the limit of visibility I used the corner of my mouth to Smith.

"Hold your breath and help me out." Maybe he did, at that. "Motors. I'll try to get the motors first."

The slapping of the salty waves against the cruiser's armored hull seemed to pause in midstride. Nothing happened—nothing, until the waves, with a frustrated sigh, gave in and began again their toppling roll and hiss. Then slowly, ever so slowly, so faintly that it was only a speck in the sky, the distant dot tilted and hung suspended on a wingtip, hung, hung, hung... A jerk, and a warped spiral. My ears rang, and the falling leaf, now swooping and sailing in agonized humpbacked scallops, seemed to double and triple in my tear-swimming eyes. Then I tried...

There was no sound. There was no booming roar, no thunder. But I forgot to yank down those dark filters over the ends of the Zeiss. They had told me that it would be like looking at the sun. Well, the sun won't throw you flat on your back, or maybe I fell. Not quite flat; Smith threw a block as I reeled, and held me upright. I tried to tell him that I was all right, that it was just the sudden glare that paralyzed me, and to get his arms off my neck before I strangled. No attention did I get from him at all in that respect, but plenty of other unneeded help. Wriggle and swear as I might, with that helmet scoring a raw groove in my neck, I was toted below and dropped on my bunk with, I suppose, what whoever carried me would call gentleness.

The anxious officer in front of me, when the action was over, had the physician's harried look. He liked my language not one little bit, and only Smith's authority kept him from calling corpsmen to muzzle me while he examined my eyes. When my sore eyes had accustomed themselves to the dim light in the cabin, Smith led the officer to the door of the hatch or whatever they call it, explaining that the recalcitrant patient would doubtless be later in a more receptive mood.

"If you think so," I yelled at his indignant ramrod back, "you must try sticking in your head and see what happens." I don't like anyone to poke anything in my eyes anytime.

Smith shut the door quickly. "Must you bellow like that? He was trying to help you."

I knew that, but I was mad. "I don't want any help. I could have made it down here under my own power, and you know it."

Smith sat down. "These your cigarettes? Thanks." He lit his own and puffed furiously. "I don't think you can reasonably expect to be let alone, Peter. After all, you're a very valuable—"

"—piece of property. Sure. In the meantime I don't want anyone fooling around me."

He smoked in silence, thinking. That meant trouble.

"Well?"

"Well, what?"

He reached for the ashtray. "Ready to talk now?"

"Sure," I said. "Talk or listen?"

"A little of both."

I talk too much. It would do me no harm to listen. "Shoot."

"This, then, Peter, is the situation; you, without a doubt, are the most remarkable person in the whole wide world. Almost an institution in yourself."

I grinned. "Like the Maine farmer; a character."

"Right. As far as I, and anyone else that has had any contact with you at all, can tell or even guess, you are absolutely and perfectly unique."

"You said that before."

"So I did. You know..." And he held my eye steadily. "...you're so completely unique, and so—dangerous, that more than once I have been personally tempted to arrange your—elimination. From behind."

I couldn't put up more than a weak grin for that. I had wondered about that, myself. A variation, a deadly one, of the old "if you can't lick 'em, join 'em" theme. And I hadn't been too cooperative.

He went on, slowly. "My personal reactions, for obvious reasons, do not enter into this. But I think, Peter, that you should consider those words very seriously before you are tempted to do or say anything rash."

I agreed that he was probably right, and that it might be better if I piped a quiet tune. "But that's not the way I operate. As far as I'm concerned, I'm responsible to myself, and myself alone. If I wanted to be told what to say and what to think, and when to say it, I would have stayed in when I got my discharge."

He shrugged. "It might be better for all concerned if you were under military discipline, although it might not suit your ego. Take, for example, the two generals you met in Detroit; Generals Hayes and Van Dorf. They both are regarded as brilliant; they are both regarded as too mentally precocious to be risked in physical action. They are two of the most agile minds on the staff."

I took his word for it. "They are still generals to me. And I don't have to stand at attention, and I don't have to take their orders."

"Exactly," and he reached for the cigarettes again. "It is not going to do any good by adding more fuel to your mental furnace, but it is only fair to tell you that the...elimination thing was more or less seriously discussed before you left Detroit."

He didn't give me a chance to blow up, but raced on. "General Hayes and General Van Dorf are sensible men, dealing in material and sensible things. You are neither practical or sensible, in many ways, this being one. They, as well equipped as they are, are not prepared to cope with such a problem presented with such as you. I might add here, that neither is anyone else. What are you laughing at?"

I couldn't help it. "The military mind at its best. First cross up the world by getting a weapon with no defense. Then when someone comes up with a defense for any weapon, including the weapon with no defense, they start turning back flips."

"Take that idiotic grin off your face." Just the same, he thought it was rather comic, himself. "Neither of us are in the Armed Forces, so for the present we can talk and plan freely. If you think, Peter, that all this can be solved with prejudice and a smart remark, you're very, very wrong. The worst is yet to come."

I asked him if I'd had a bed of roses, so far. "I don't think I could be much worse off than I've been so far. How would you like to be penned up—"

"Penned up?" He snorted disgustedly. "You've had yourself a holiday, and you can't see it. Try to see the military, the legal point of view. Here is one person, Peter Ambrose Miller, one man and only one man, with the ability, the power, to cancel at one stroke every scientific advancement that armament has made in the past three thousand years."

"And the big boys don't like it," I mused.

"The little boys, as you use the word, won't like it, either," he said. "But, that's not the point. Not the point at all. The stem of the apple is this—what are we going to do with you?"

"We?" I asked him.

"We," he explained carefully, as to a baby, "is a generic term for the army, the navy, the government, the world in general. As long as you live, as long as you continue to be able to do the things you can do now, a gun or an airplane is so much scrap metal. But—only as long as you live!"

That I didn't like. "You mean that—"

"Exactly what I said. As long as you're alive a soldier or a sailor might as well be a Zulu; useful for the length he can throw a spear or shoot an arrow, but useless as he now stands. There is no army, apparently, right now that is worth more than its body weight—again, as long as you live."

"Do you have to harp on that?"

"Why not? Do you want to live forever, or do you expect to?"

He had me there. You bet I wanted to live forever. "Well?"

He yanked pensively at his upper lip. "Two solutions; one, announce you to the world with a clang of cymbals and a roll of drums. Two, bury you someplace. Oh, figuratively speaking," he added hastily as he saw my face.

"Solution one sounds good to me," I told him. "I could go home then."

He made it quite clear that Solution One was only theoretical; he was firm about that. "Outside of rewriting all the peace treaties in existence, do you remember how our Congress huddled over the Bomb? Can you see Congress allowing you, can you see the General Staff agreeing to share you with, for example, a United Nations Commission? Can you?"

No, I couldn't.

"So," with a regretful sigh, "Solution One leaves only Solution Two. We'll grant that you must be kept under cover."

I wondered if Stein was somewhere at the earphones of a tape recorder. For someone with as big a job as the old man likely had, it seemed that we were talking fairly freely. He went on.

"And that Solution Two has within itself another unsolved problem; who watches you, and who watches the watchers?"

That didn't matter to me, and I said so.

"I suppose not to you, but it would matter to the army, and it would matter to the navy, and when J. Edgar Hoover gets around to thinking about it, it will matter to the FBI."

"So what? Would I get a choice?"

He was curious for a moment. "Would you want one?"

"Maybe, maybe not. I had a uniform once. The FBI go to college and take off their hats in the house, but they're still cops, and I don't like cops. Don't look at me like that; you wouldn't like cops either, if you made less than a couple of hundred a week. Nobody does. So I'm prejudiced against everybody, and just what difference does it make?"

"Not a great deal. I was just curious." He was honest, anyway. "But you can see the possibilities, or the lack of them."

"Look," and I got up to take as many steps as the cabin would allow. "This is where we came in. We could talk all day and get no further. All I want to know is this—what's going to happen to me, and when, and where?"

He followed me with his steady eyes. "Well, at the immediate moment, I'm afraid that—" He hesitated.

"I'm afraid that, quick like a bunny, you're going to have one solid headache if we don't quit using the same words over and over again. Here I am stuck in the middle of all the water in the world, and I'm tired, and I'm disgusted, and I'm starting to get mad. You're trying to smother my head in a pillow, I've got nothing but a first-class run-around from you and everyone I've seen, who has been one man named Bob Stein. I see nothing, I know less, I get cold shoulders and hot promises."

I sailed right on, not giving him a chance to slide in one word. "Why, there must be ten thousand men and maybe some women right upstairs, and who knows how many within a few miles from here, and do I get to even pass the time of day with any of them? Do I? You bet your sweet life I don't!"

"There aren't any women within miles of here, except nurses, and maybe a reporter, and I'm not sure about that."

"Nurses and reporters are human, aren't they?"

Had he found a chink in the armor? He frowned. "Is it women you want?"

"Sure, I want women!" I flared at him. "I want a million of them! I want Esther Williams and Minnie Mouse and anyone else that looks good to me. But I don't want them on a silver platter with a gilt chain. I want them when I want them—my wife and the waitress at Art's, and the beer I used to drink would taste a lot better than the beer you said I'd get and never seen!"

The Smith stood up and I sat down. "Women and beer. Anything else?"

"Sure," I snapped at him. "Women and beer and traffic piled up on Gratiot and the same double feature at all the movies in town—" I got a look at him. I felt silly. "All right, take out the needle. You win."

He was a gentleman. He didn't laugh. "Win? Yes, I suppose I win." Before I could think of anything else to say, he was gone.

PART TWO

Smith knocked early the next morning when Stein was still clearing the breakfast coffee. For that time of day he was disgustingly happy.

"The customary greeting, I believe, is good morning, is it not?"

I gulped the rest of my cup. "Yeah. What's on your mind?"

He sat down and waved away Stein's wordless offer of a cup. "How would we like to take a little trip?"

We. The editorial we. "Why not?"

"This little trip—how would you like to go back home for awhile?"

"Home?" I couldn't believe my ears, and I stared at him.

He'd made a slip, and he was sorry. "I meant, back stateside."

I slumped back in my chair. "Then you heard me the first time. What's the difference?"

"Quite a bit of difference. No, Stein, you stay here. We're all in this together."

"Sure," I said. "Stick around. I'm the last one to find out what's going on around here."

He didn't appreciate my sarcasm. "I wouldn't say that, Peter."

"Forget it. What's the story?"

"We want you to go back where we can run some tests, this time as comprehensive as we can arrange."

I couldn't see why what we'd done wouldn't be enough. "Don't tell me you have more than the Bomb up your sleeve."

No, it wasn't like that. "There aren't more than four or six that know anything but that the Bomb was set off prematurely because of motor failure on the drone. The general knowledge is that it was just another test in routine fashion. But, as I said, there are a few that know the truth. They think it desirable that you be examined scientifically, and completely."

"Why?" I felt ornery.

He knew it, and showed a little impatience. "Use your head, Peter. You know better than that. We know you're unique. We want to know why, and perhaps how, perhaps, your ability can be duplicated."

That appealed to me. "And if you can find out what makes me tick I can go back to living like myself again?" I took his silence for assent. I had to. "Good. What do I do, and when?"

He shrugged. "Nothing, yet. You'll go to…well, let's call it college. It shouldn't take too long. A week, maybe, maybe two, or four, at the most."

"Then what?"

He didn't know. We'd talk about that later. Okay with me. If a doctor could find out how I was whistling chords, all well and good. If not—could I be any worse off?

"Then it's settled. We'll leave today, if it can be arranged, and I feel sure it can. Robert…" To Stein: "…if you'll come with me we'll try to make the necessary arrangements." Stein left, and Smith left, and I got up and looked into the mirror. I needed a shave again.

MY COLLEGE didn't have a laboratory worth counting when I went to school. We'd had a stadium, and a losing football team instead. Now the balding, bearded physicists sat in the front row when the appropriations were spooned out. I suppose that's all for the better. I really wouldn't know. The old fellow that met us at the front door looked like an Airedale, and like an Airedale he sniffed all around me before getting into combat range.

"So you're Peter Miller!"

"That's my name," I admitted. I wondered what all the dials and the gadgets were for. It looked to me like the front end of one of these computers I used to see in the magazines.

"I'm Kellner. You must be Stein, right? Never mind your coats. Just follow me," and off he trotted, and we trailed him into a bare office with what looked like the equipment of a spendthrift dentist.

"You sit here," and he waved at a straight-backed chair. I sat down, Stein shifted nervously from one foot to the other, and in a moment Kellner came back with a dozen others. He didn't bother to introduce any of them. They all stood off and gaped at who'd killed Cock Robin.

Kellner broke the silence. "Physical first?" There was a general nod. "Physical, psychological, then—we'll come to that later." To Stein: "Want to come along? Rather wait here? This is going to take some time, you know."

Stein knew that. He also wanted to come along. Those were his orders.

I felt self-conscious taking off my clothes in front of that ghoulish crew. The sheet they left me kept off no drafts, and I felt like a corpse ready for the embalmer, and likely appeared one. Stethoscope, a scale for my weight, a tape for my arm and the blood pressure, lights that blinked in my eyes and bells that rang in my ear...when they were finished with me I felt like a used Tinker-Toy.

"Do I pass? Will I live?"

Kellner didn't like juvenile humor. He turned me over to another group who, so help me, brought out a box of children's blocks to put together, timing me with a stopwatch. They used the same stopwatch to time how long it took me to come up with answers to some of the silliest questions I ever heard outside of a nursery. Now I know why they label well the patients in an insane asylum. The man with the watch galloped off and came back with Kellner and they all stood around muttering. The sheet and I were sticking to the chair.

"Kellner. Doctor Kellner!" They didn't like me to break up the kaffeeklatch. "Can I go now? Are you all through?"

"All through?" The Airedale changed to a cackling Rhode Island Red. "Joseph, you are just beginning."

"My name isn't Joseph, Dr. Kellner. It's Miller. Peter Ambrose Miller."

"Excuse me, Peter," and he cackled again. "Nevertheless, you're going to be here quite awhile."

Peter, hey? No more, Mr. Miller. Pete to my wife, Peter to my mother, and Peter to every school teacher I ever had.

They conferred awhile longer and the party broke up. Kellner and a gawkish Great Dane led me sheet and all to what I thought would be the operating room. It looked like one. I found a chair all by myself this time, and watched them hook up an electric fan. They were hipped on fans, I thought.

Kellner trotted over. "Stop that fan." Not, please stop that fan. Just, stop that fan.

I shivered ostentatiously. "I'm cold."

Kellner was annoyed. "Perfectly comfortable in here." Sure, you old goat, you got your pants on. "Come, let's not delay. Stop the fan."

I told him I was still cold, and I looked at the fan. It threw sparks, and the long cord smoked. I was going to fix those boys.

The other man yanked the cord from the wall, and from the way he sucked his fingers, it must have been hot. Kellner was pleased at that. He ignored the man's sore fingers and snarled at him until he brought out some dry cells and hooked them in series to a large bell, almost a gong. He pressed the button and it clanged.

"All right," and Kellner motioned imperiously to me. "No point in fooling. We know you can make it stop ringing. Now, go ahead and ring the bell."

I looked at him. "Make the bell ring what?"

"What?" He was genuinely puzzled. "What's this?"

"I said make the bell ring what?" He stared blankly at me. "And you heard me the first time!" He shot an astonished glance at Stein. "Oh, hell!" I got up and started out, trailing my sheet. I almost stumbled over Stein, who was right at my shoulder.

"Here, what's this?" Kellner was bouncing with excitement.

I turned on him. "Listen you; I said I was cold. Not once, but twice I said I was cold. Now, blast it, I want my clothes, and I want them now. Right now!" The Airedale became a fish out of water. "Do I look like a ten-year-old in to get his tonsils out? I ask you a civil question and you smirk at me, you tell me to do this and you tell me to do that and never a please or a thank you or a kiss my foot. Don't pull that Doctor write the prescription in Latin on me, because I don't like it! Catch?" Stein was right on my heel when I headed for the door.

Poor Stein was wailing aloud. "Pete, you can't do this! Don't you know who Doctor Kellner is?"

"One big healthy pain!" I snapped at him. "Does he know who I am? I'm Pete Miller, Mister Miller to him or to anyone but my friends. I want my pants!"

Stein wrung his hands and slowed me down as much as I would let him. "You just can't get up and walk out like that!"

"Oh, no?" I came to a full stop and leered at him. "Who's going to stop me?"

That's the trouble with the doctors and lawyers and technical boys; they're so used to talking over people's heads they can't answer a civil question in less than forty syllables. Keep all the secrets in the trade. Write it in Latin, keep the patient in the dark, pat his head and tell him papa knows best.

When Kellner caught up with us he had help. "Here, here, my man. Where do you think you are going?"

I wished he was my age and forty pounds heavier. "Me? I'm getting out of here. And I'm not your man and I never will be. When you can admit that, and not act like I'm a set of chalk marks on a blackboard, send me a letter and tell me about it. One side, dogface!"

One big fellow, just the right size, puffed out his cheeks. "Just whom do you think you are addressing?"

Whom. I looked him over. I never did like people who wore van Dyke goatees. I put whom and van Dyke on the floor. It was a good Donnybrook while it lasted. The last thing I remember was the gong in the next room clanging steadily while Stein, good old Stein, right in there beside me was swinging and yelling, "Don't hurt him! Don't hurt him!"

I woke up with another headache. When I sat up with a grunt and looked around I saw Stein and his nose four inches from a mirror, gingerly trying his tongue against his front teeth. I snickered. He didn't like that, and turned around.

"You don't look so hot yourself."

He was right. I couldn't see much out of my left eye. We grinned at each other. "Right in there pitching, weren't you?"

He shrugged. "What did you expect me to do?"

"Run for help," I told him. "Or stand there and watch me get a going over."

"Sure." He looked uncomfortable. "I'm supposed to keep an eye on you."

"So you did." I thought back. "What happened to Whom when I addressed him properly?"

It must have hurt his cheek when he tried to smile. "Still out, at last report. You know, Pete, you have a fairly good left—and a lousy temper."

I knew that. "I just got tired of getting pushed around. Besides, with no pants I was stuck to that chair."

"Probably." His tongue pushed gently against his sore lip. "You think that was the right way to go about making things better?"

Maybe not. But did he have any better ideas?

He wasn't sure, but he didn't think a laboratory was just the right place for a brawl.

"Just why I started it. Now what?"

He didn't know that either. "Kellner is having hysterics, and I just made some phone calls."

If the Old Man showed up I had some nice words ready to use. "Now we might get some action."

Stein gave me a sour look. "Not necessarily the kind you'll like. I'll be back after I try to talk some sense into Kellner."

"Hey!" I yelled after him. "Where's my pants?"

"Back in a few minutes," he tossed over his shoulder; "make yourself comfortable," and he left.

COMFORTABLE WITH a cot and a mirror and a washbowl. I washed my face and lay on the cot with a washrag soaked in cold water on my throbbing eye. I must have dozed off. When I woke the Old Man was standing over me. I sat up and the rag fell off my eye.

"What's cooking, Bossman?"

I don't think his frown was completely genuine. "You, apparently."

I swung my legs over the edge of the cot and stretched. "Have a seat and a cigarette."

He sat down beside me and reached for his lighter. "Peter, I wish—"

I cut in on him. "Item one, I want my pants."

He gestured impatiently. "You'll get them. Now—"

"I said, I want my pants."

He began to get annoyed. "I told you—"

"And I told you I want my pants. I don't want them later or in a while; I want my pants and I want them now."

He sat back and looked at me. "What's all this?"

I let fly. "For the record, I want my pants. I'm certainly no patient in this morgue, and I'm not going to be treated like one, so whatever you or anyone else has got to say to me is not going to be while I'm as bare as a baby. My mind's made up," and I scrunched together ungracefully on the little space that remained on my end of the cot and pulled the sheet over my head. Kid stuff, and we both knew it.

He didn't say anything, although I could feel his eyes boring through the flimsy sheet, and I lay there until I felt the springs creak as he got up and I could hear his footsteps retreating. When he came back with my clothes over his arm I was sitting up. While I was dressing he tried to talk to me, but I would have none of it.

When I was dressed I said, "Now, you were saying—?"

I drew a long speculative stare. "Peter, what's eating you?"

I told him. "I just got tired of being shoved around. With the physical exam over with you give me one reason why I should sit around in my bare hide. Am I a machine? My name's Miller, not the Patient in Cell Two."

He thought he was being reasonable. "And you think you get results by knocking around people who try to help you?"

"With some people, you do. I tried talking, and that didn't work. I got action my way, didn't I?"

He sighed. "Action, yes. Do you know what Kellner said?"

"Not interested. Whatever he's got to say to me is going to have a please in front and a thank you after."

Wearily, "Peter, must you always act like a child?"

"No, I don't," I blazed at him. "But I'm damn well going to. I'm free, white and a citizen, and I'm going to be treated like one, and not a side-show freak!"

"Now, now," he soothed. "Doctor Kellner is a very famous and a very busy man. He might not have realized—"

"Realize your hat! He's so used to living in the clouds he thinks the world is one big moron. Well, I may be one, but no one is going to tell me I am!"

"I see your point," and he stood up. "But you try to be a little more cooperative. I'll see Kellner now," and he started out.

"Cooperative?" I bellowed at his back. "What do you think I've been doing? What do you—"

He must have read the riot act. When they took me in to Kellner and his crew it was "please, Mr. Miller" and "thank you, Mr. Miller." The place didn't seem so cold and bare so long as I had my pants. I didn't see Whom and his van Dyke, but I hoped it was the tile floor and not me that gave him the concussion.

The rest of the tests, you can imagine, were almost anticlimactic. I stopped motors, blew tubes, turned lights off and on, rang bells and cooked the insulation on yards and yards of wire. My head they kept connected with taped terminals and every time I blew a fuse or a motor they would see the dials spin crazily. Then they would stand around clucking and chattering desperately. They took X-rays by the score, hoping to find something wrong with the shape of my head, and for all the results they got, might have been using a Brownie on a cue ball. Then they'd back off to the corner and sulk. One little bearded rascal, in particular, to this day is certain that Kellner was risking his life in getting within ten feet. He never turned his back on me that I recall; he sidled around, afraid I would set his watch to running backwards. You know, one of the funniest and yet one of the most pathetic things in the world is the spectacle of someone who has spent his life in mastering a subject, only to find that he has built a sled without runners. Long before we were finished I thought Kellner, for one, was going to eat his tie, stripes and all. Running around in ever-widening circles they were, like coon dogs after a scent. They didn't get a smell. The medico who ran the electro-cardiograph refused to make sense, after the fifth trials, out of the wiggly marks on his graphs.

"Kellner," he stated flatly, "I don't know just what your game is, but these readings are not true."

Kellner didn't like that. Nor did he like the man who wanted to shave my head. I wouldn't let them do that. I look bad enough now. I compromised by letting them soak my head in what smelled like water, and then tying or pasting strands of tape all over my scalp. A pretty mess I was, as bad as a woman getting a permanent wave. Worse. One whole day I stood for that. This specialist, whatever he did, had Kellner get me to run through my repertoire of bells and fans and buzzers while he peered nearsightedly at his elaborate tool shop. When the fuse would blow or the bell would ring, the specialist would wince as though he were pinched. Kellner stood over his shoulder saying at intervals, "What do you get? What do you get?" Kellner finally got it. The specialist stood up, swore in Platt-deutsch, some at Kellner and some at me and some at his machine, and left in all directions. The gist of it was that he was too important and too busy to have jokes played on him. Kellner just wagged his head and walked out.

The Old Man said, "You're not one bit different from anyone else."

"Sure," I said. "I could have told you that long ago. It shouldn't take a doctor."

"Miller, what in blazes are we going to do with you?"

I didn't know. I'd done my share. "Where do we go from here?"

The Old Man looked out the window. The sun was going down. "Someone wants to see you. He's been waiting for Kellner to finish with you. We leave tonight."

"For where?" I didn't like this running around. "Who's 'he'?"

"For Washington. You'll see who it is."

Washington, more than just a sleeper jump away. Washington? Oh, oh... Well, let's get it over with. We did. We left for the capital that night.

We slipped in the back door, or what passed for the back door. Pretty elaborate layout, the White House. Our footsteps rang as hollow as my heart on the shiny waxed floors.

The Old Man did the honors. "Mr. President, this is Mr. Miller."

He shook hands. He had a good grip.

"General Hayes, you know. Admiral Lacey, Admiral Jessop, Mr. Hoover you know, General Buckley. Gentlemen. Mr. Miller."

We shook hands all around. "Glad to know you." My palms were slippery.

The President sat, and we followed suit. The guest of honor, I felt like my head was shaved, and I had a slit pants leg. You don't meet the President every day.

The President broke the ice. It was thin to begin with. "You have within yourself the ability, the power, to do a great deal for your country, Mr. Miller, or would you prefer to be called Pete?"

Pete was all right. He was older, and bigger. Bigger all around.

"A great deal of good, or a great deal of harm."

No harm. I'm a good citizen.

"I'm sure of that. But you can understand what I mean, by harm."

Likely I could, if I really wanted to. But I didn't. Not the place where you were born.

"Naturally, Pete, it makes me feel a great deal better, however, to hear you say and phrase it just like that." The light of the lamp glittered on his glasses. "Very, very much better, Pete."

I was glad it was dark beyond the range of the lamp. My face was red. "Thank you, Mr. President."

"I like it better, Pete, because from this day on, Pete, you and I and all of us know that you, and you alone, are going to have a mighty hard row to hoe." That's right; he was a farmer once. "Hard in this respect—you understand, I know, that for the rest of your natural life you must and shall be guarded with all the alert fervor that national security demands. Does that sound too much like a jail sentence?"

It did, but I lied. I said, "Not exactly, Mr. President. Whatever you say is all right with me."

He smiled. "Thank you, Pete... Guarded as well and as closely as—the question is, where?"

I didn't know I'd had a choice. The Old Man had talked to me before on that.

"Not exactly, Pete. This is what I mean: General Buckley and General Hayes feel that you will be safest on the mainland somewhere in the Continental United States. Admirals Lacey and Jessop, on the other hand, feel that the ever-present risk of espionage can be controlled only by isolation, perhaps on some island where the personnel can be exclusively either military or naval."

I grinned inwardly. I knew this was going to happen.

"Mr. Hoover concedes that both possible places have inherent advantages and disadvantages," the President went on. "He feels, however, that protection should be provided by a staff specially trained in law-enforcement and counter-espionage."

So where did that leave me? I didn't say it quite that way, but I put across the idea.

The President frowned a bit at nothing. "I'm informed you haven't been too...comfortable."

I gulped. Might as well be hung for a sheep. If the Boss likes you, the Help must. "I'm sorry, Mr. President, but it isn't much fun being shifted around pillar and post."

He nodded slowly. "Quite understandable, under the circumstances. That, we'll try to eliminate as much as we can. You can see, Pete," and he flashed that famous wide grin, "it will be in the national interest to see that you are always in the finest physical and mental condition. Crudely expressed, perhaps, but the truth, nevertheless."

I like people to tell me the truth. He could see that. He's like that, himself. On his job, you have to be like that.

"Now, Pete; let's get down to cases. Have you any ideas, any preferences, any suggestions?" He took a gold pencil out of his breast pocket and it began to twirl.

I had an idea, all right. "Why not just let me go back home? I'll keep my mouth shut, I won't blow any fuses or raise any hell, if you'll excuse the expression."

Someone coughed. The President turned his head out of the circle of light. "Yes, Mr. Hoover?"

J. Edgar Hoover was diffident. "Er...Mrs. Miller has been informed of her husband's...demise. An honorable one," he hastened to add, "and is receiving a comfortable pension, paid from the Bureau's special funds."

"How much?" I wanted to know.

He shifted uncomfortably. "Well...a hundred a month."

I looked at the President. "Bought any butter lately?"

The President strangled a cough. "Have you, Mr. Hoover, bought any butter lately?"

J. Edgar Hoover couldn't say anything. It wasn't his fault.

I flicked a glance at General Hayes. "How much does it cost the Army for an antiaircraft gun?" I looked at one of the admirals. "And how much goes down the drain when you launch a battleship? Or even a PT boat?"

The President took over. "Rest assured, Mr. Miller. Your wife's pension is quadrupled, effective immediately." He swung his chair to face Hoover; "Cash will be transferred tomorrow to the Bureau from the State Department's special fund. You'll see to that?" to the Old Man. So that was what he did for a living. That State Department is a good lifetime job, I understand.

That took a load from my mind, but not all. I spoke to Hoover directly.

"How is my...widow?"

As tense and as bad as I felt just then, I was sorry for him.

"Quite well, Mr. Miller. Quite well, considering. It came as a blow to her, naturally—"

"What about the house?" I asked him. "Is she keeping up the payments?"

He had to admit that he didn't know. The President told him to finish the payments, pay for the house. Over and above the pension? Over and above the pension. And I was to get a regular monthly report on how she was getting along.

"Excuse me, Mr. President. I'd rather not get a regular monthly report, or any word at all, unless she—unless anything happens to her."

"No report at all, Pete?" That surprised, him, and he eyed me over the top of his bifocals.

"She's still young, Mr. President," I said, "and she's just as pretty as the day we got married. I don't think I'd want to know if...she got married again."

The quiet was thick enough to slice. If they talked about Helen any more I was going to throw something. The President saw how I felt.

"Now, Mr. Miller—Pete. Let's get back to business. You were saying—?"

Yes, I had an idea. "Put me on an island somewhere, the further away the better. I wouldn't like being around things without being able to be in the middle. Better put me where I can't weaken, where I can't sneak out a window or swim back." Everyone was listening. "Keep the uniforms away from me, out of sight." The Brass didn't like that, but they heard me out. "Feed me a case of beer once in a while and a few magazines and some books and right boys to play euchre. I guess that's all I want."

The gold pencil turned over and over. "That isn't very much, Pete."

"That's all. If I'm going to do the Army's and the Navy's work they can leave me alone till they need me. If I can't live my life the way I want, it makes no difference what I do. My own fault is that all my family lived to be eighty, and so will I. Is that what you wanted to know?"

The gold pencil rolled off the table. "Yes, yes, Pete. That's what I wanted to know."

I tried once more. "There isn't any way I can just go home?"

A slow shake of his head, and finality was in his voice. "I'm afraid there isn't any way." And that was that.

The President stood up in dismissal, and we all rose nervously. He held out his hand. "Sorry, Pete. Perhaps some day..."

I shook his hand limply and the Old Man was at my elbow to steer me out. Together we paced back through the dark hall, together we stepped quietly out into the black Washington night. Our footsteps echoed softly past the buildings of the past and the future. The car was waiting; Stein, the driver. The heavy door slammed, and the tires hissed me from the pavement.

The Old Man's voice was gentle. "You behaved well, Peter."

"Yeah."

"I was afraid, for a moment, that you were going to kick over the traces. The President is a very important man."

"Yeah."

"You are, too. Right now, probably the most important man in the world. You took it very well."

"Yeah."

"Is that all you have to say?"

I looked out the window. "Yeah," and he fell quiet.

Stein got us to the airport, and there was waiting an Army ship for the three of us. I might have been able to see the Monument or the Capitol when we were airborne. I don't know. I didn't look.

Later I asked Stein where we were going. He didn't know. I prodded the Old Man out of a doze. I wished I could sleep.

He hesitated. Then, "West. Far west."

"West." I thought that over. "How much out of your way would it be to fly over Detroit?"

"You couldn't see much."

I knew that. "How much out of your way?"

Not too much. He nodded to Stein, who got up and went forward. After he came back and sat down the plane slipped on one wing and straightened on its new course. No one said anything more after that.

We hit Detroit about five thousand feet, the sun just coming up from Lake Ste. Clair. Smith was right. Although I craned my neck I couldn't see much. I picked up Gratiot, using the Penobscot Tower for a landmark, and followed it to Mack, and out Mack. I could just pick out the dogleg at Connors, and imagined I could see the traffic light at Chalmers. I had to imagine hard. The way we were flying, the body and the wing hid where I'd lived, where—the cigarette I had in my fist tasted dry, and so did my mouth, so I threw it down and closed my eyes and tried to sleep. Somewhere around Nebraska we landed for fuel.

MAYBE IT was Kansas. It was flat, and hot, and dry. The Old Man and Stein and I got out to stretch our legs. There was no shade, no trees, no green oasis for the traveler. The olive drab tanker that pulled up to pump gas into our wing tanks was plastered with "No Smoking" tabs, and we walked away before the hose was fully unreeled. Off to our right was the only shade, back of the landing strip, a great gray hangar glutted with shiny-nosed, finny monsters. Out of the acrid half-pleasant reek of high-octane, we stood smoking idly, watching the denimed air-crews clamber fly-like over the jutting wings. From the post buildings off to the right jounced a dusty motorcycle. We watched it twist to a jerking stop at our refueling ship, and the soldier that dismounted bobbed in salute to the two pilots watching the gassing operation. Two motions only they used; one to return the salute and another to point us out in the shadow of the hangar. The soldier shaded his eyes from the sun to peer in our direction, calculated the distance with his eye, and then roared his motorcycle almost to our feet.

"Post Commander's compliments," he barked. "And will the gentlemen please report at once to the Colonel's office?"

The Old Man eyed the motorcycle and the empty sidecar. He looked at Stein.

"Better stay here," he said thoughtfully. "If I need you, I'll come back." He climbed awkwardly into the sidecar, and the soldier, after a hesitant acceptance, kicked the starter. The Old Man gripped the sides firmly as they bounced away in the baking breeze, and Stein looked absently at his watch. It was close to noon.

At twelve-thirty the gas truck rolled ponderously back to its den. At one, our two pilots struck out across the strip for the post buildings, shimmering in the heat. At one-thirty, I turned to Stein, who had been biting his nails for an hour.

"Enough is enough," I said. "Who finds out what—you or I?"

He hesitated, and strained his eyes. The Old Man, nor anyone, was not in sight. The post might have been alone in the Sahara. He chewed his lip.

"Me, I guess." He knew better than to argue with me, in my mood. "I'll be back. Ten minutes," and he started for the post. He got no further than half the distance when an olive sedan, a big one, raced toward us. It stopped for Stein, sucked him into the front seat, whirled back past me to our plane standing patiently, and dumped out our two pilots. A final abrupt bounding spin brought it to the hangar. The Old Man leaned out of the back door.

"In, quick," he snapped.

I got in, and the soldier driver still had the sedan in second gear when we got to our ship. One motor was already coughing, and as we clambered into the cabin the starter caught the second. Both propellers vanished into a silvered arc, and without a preparatory warm-up we slewed around and slammed back in the bucket seats in a pounding takeoff. Stein went forward to the pilot's cabin, and I turned, half-angrily, to the Smith. His face was etched with bitterness. Something was wrong, something seriously wrong.

"What's up?" I asked. "What's the big hurry?"

He flicked a sidelong glance at me, and his brows almost met. He looked mad, raving mad.

"Well?" I said. "Cat got your tongue?" I noticed then that he was fraying and twisting a newspaper. I hadn't seen a newspaper for what seemed years. Stein came back and sat on the edge of the seat. What in blazes was the matter?

Smith said something unprintable. That didn't sound right, coming from that refined face. I raised my eyebrows.

"Leak," he ended succinctly. "There's been a leak. The word's out!"

That was a surprise. A big one.

"And it's thanks to you!"

"Me?"

He flipped the newspaper at me. I caught it in midair, and there it was, smeared all over the face of the Kansas City *Sentinel*. Great, black, tall shrieking streamer heads:

AMERICA HAS ATOMIC DEFENSE!

I scanned the two columns of stumbling enthusiastic prose that trailed over on to Page Two. Stein came over and leaned over my shoulder and breathed on my ear as we read. He hadn't seen the sheet, either. It ran something like this:

America, it was learned today, has at last an absolute defense, not only to the atomic bomb, but to every gun, every airplane, every engine, every weapon capable of being used by man. Neither admitted nor denied at this early date by even the highest government officials, it was learned by our staff late last night that America's latest step forward...

Column after column of stuff like that. When the reporter got through burbling, he did have a few facts that were accurate. He did say it was my doing that set off the last atomic bomb test; he did say that I was apparently invulnerable to violence powered by electrical or internal combustion engines; he did say what I could do, and what I had done, and how often. He didn't say who I was, or what I looked like, or where I'd come from, or what I did or didn't know.

Sprinkled through the story—and I followed it back to Page 32 and the pictures rehashed of the traffic jam in Detroit—were references to T. Sylvester Colquhoun, the boy who dumped the original plate of beans. He attested this and swore to that. Whoever he was, wherever he got his information, he—there was his picture on Page 32, big as life and twice as obnoxious; Mr. Whom and the van Dyke.

Guiltily I handed the paper over to Stein, who turned back to the front page and started again from the beginning. I tried to carry things off in the nonchalant manner, but I couldn't. I had to watch the Old Man light a cigarette with fumbling fingers, take a few snorting puffs, and crush it viciously under his heel. Miller and his temper.

Whom—or T. Sylvester Colquhoun—had, very obviously, a grudge against the short left that had given him his concussion. According to the *Sentinel*, he had babbled a bit when he was released from the hospital, and an alert newshawk had trailed him to his home and bluffed him into spilling the whole story. He had sense enough, at that late stage of the game, to keep my name out of it, if he ever knew it. The reporter had gone to his editor with the story, who had laughed incredulously at first, and then checked Kellner at the laboratory. Kellner had clammed up, and when the now suspicious editor had tried to check Colquhoun's tale personally, Colquhoun had vanished. A snooping neighbor had noted the license of the car that had taken him away. The Highway Department—the editor must have moved fast and decisively—showed the license plate as issued to a man the editor knew personally as a special agent of the Kansas City Branch of the FBI.

Then hell began to pop. Repeated long-distance calls to Washington ran him up against a stone wall. The answers he got convinced him that there was something to Colquhoun's wild tale, something weird and yet something that had a germ of truth. (Half of this, understand, was in the *Sentinel.* The other half I picked up later on, adding two and two.) As he was sitting mulling things over it was his turn to get a call from Washington. The State Department was on the line; Morgan, the Under Secretary.

Morgan fairly yelled at him. "Where did you get that information? What's the idea?" and so on. That clinched it for the editor. Then it was he knew.

Morgan made his mistake there. He began to threaten, and the editor hit the ceiling. Hit it hard, because he stretched things a little. He stretched it more than just a little.

He said, "Furthermore, that's on the street right now—this is a newspaper, not a morgue!"

It wasn't on the street, the editor knew. Perhaps he wanted to throw a scare into Morgan, perhaps—But Morgan!

Morgan gasped, "Oh, my God!" and hung up with a bang.

The editor flipped a mental coin. His circulation was not what it should be, the boss had been riding him lately, his job might be where a beat would tilt the balance up or down. The national safety that Morgan had shouted about—well, if we had the perfect weapon and the perfect defense, what was there to fear? And this *was* a newspaper, not a morgue! They redid the plates, and the first extras hit the street to wake up half the city. The wire services had the story and extras were rolling throughout the country, or the world, about the time I was watching the sun over Lake Ste. Clair.

Neither the State Department nor the FBI were on their toes that day. Instead of denying everything, or instead of laughing heartily at the pipedream of an editor trying to sell an extra edition or two, whoever was pulling the strings behind the scenes demanded flatly that all wire services kill and disregard all references to Colquhoun. No one ever made a newspaperman do what he really didn't want to do. The very fact that the government was so eager to kill the story made every newsman worthy of his salt all the more eager to break the paper-thin shell around the meaty yolk. By noon, the time we landed for fuel, every Washington correspondent for every news service had a little different story for his boss, the White House was practically besieged at the mere rumor that the President was to issue a statement, and the State Department was going quietly mad.

"Not so quietly, at that," the Old Man said sourly. "One hour straight I stayed on that telephone. One hour straight I talked to one bunch of raving maniacs, and all the common sense I heard would go into your left eye."

By that time his temper had cooled below melting, and we were again on reasonably good terms. I was curious to know just who the Old Man had talked to.

He grunted. "Just about everyone in Washington with any authority at all. No one with any intelligence."

I could appreciate that. I have a very low opinion of anyone who stays in Washington any longer than necessary.

I asked him, "We're apparently heading back there. Why? Where were we going when they stopped us?"

He wasn't sure. "I wanted to keep on going," he said, "and get you out of the country. I still think that would have been best. There was to be a cruiser waiting at Bremerton for a shakedown cruise. But whoever is running all this—and I don't think that the President has thought too much about it—wants us to get back to Washington for another conference."

"Another meeting?" I was disgusted. Washington political rashes manifest themselves most often by the consistent eruption of conferences in which nothing is said, nothing decided, nothing done. "What does who think what?"

He blinked, and then smiled. "I couldn't say. I've been in this game only twenty years. At any rate, you can see who's worried."

I didn't see, exactly.

"No?" He was amused. "Don't you remember the discussion we had about who was going to watch the watchers? Now that there's been a leak, the Army is going to blame the Navy, the Navy is going to blame the FBI, and I take punishment from all three." He sighed. "My department seems, invariably, to be in the middle."

I let it go at that. I didn't have the heart to remind him that a good portion of the trouble and friction this country has had in its history has been because the State Department has been sitting on the water bucket when it should have been playing deep centerfield. No use worrying about things until the fuse is burnt half its length, I thought. That might be, for me and all of us, a good policy to adopt, for the time being. Let the boys at the top fret and worry; let them wrack their brains and beat their heads against the wall. I'd do what they told me, if I could. The man that pays the salary worries about the unemployment tax.

"Stein," I said, "are there any more of those sandwiches?"

The Old Man settled back in his seat and began to read the Kansas City *Sentinel* all over again. He was still worried when we landed in Washington.

He left in a waiting black sedan, and Stein and I stayed in the ship until it was yanked into a dark hangar by a tiny tractor with great rubber tires. We slid out the back of the hangar when the wary Stein thought it was safe, and a taxi rolled us to the Mayflower. There we registered, I was told, as James Robertson and William Wakefield, Wisconsin Dells.

"Milwaukee," I suggested, "has better beer."

He took the hint, and when the waiter brought our late dinner, the ice bucket had eight frosty bottles. They practically sizzled when they went down. Bob Stein, at times, had some earmarks of genius, even if you had to lay them bare with an axe.

The first day wasn't bad; we sat around, drank beer and ate huge sirloins on the swindle sheet, and told all the stories we knew. The radio was blurting either soap operas, hillbilly music, or lentil-mouthed commentators. The story broken in the *Sentinel* was gathering momentum, by what we read and heard, and that was too close to home. So we made a pact to turn off the radio and keep it that way. We never missed it.

The second day the beer tasted as good as ever. The steaks were just as thick and just as tender, the hotel service just as unobtrusive. Stein was just as cheerful and as pleasant company. But I spent a lot of time looking out the window.

"You know, Bob," I said thoughtfully, "how would you like a big plate of spaghetti? Or ravioli? Maybe some pizza?"

He came out of the bathroom wiping his face with a towel, his hair wet and frizzled.

"Am I going to have trouble with you?" He was pessimistic. "Aren't you ever satisfied?"

I turned away from the window and let the curtain flap in the breeze. "Who wants to be satisfied? How about some sub-gum war mein, or chicken cacciatora?"

He tossed the towel back through the open door. "Now, look here," he protested.

I laughed at him. "Okay, but you get the point."

He did, but he didn't know what he could do about it. "We were supposed to wait here until—"

That one I'd heard before. "Until the hotel freezes over, sure. But I don't want to freeze. Do you?"

No, nor to rust. You could see that he liked his job of body-guard and factotum, and yet...

I pushed him over the edge. "Tell you what to do," I said. "You call up and say that I'm getting restless. Say that you're afraid and I'll ease out of here when your back is turned. Say

anything you like, as long as you lay it on thick, and I'll back you up. Okay?"

He weighed it awhile. He liked inaction, no matter how sybaritic as much as I. Then, "Okay," and he reached for the telephone.

The number he gave answered the first ring.

"I'm calling for Mr. Robertson," he said. "This is Mr. William Wakefield. W. W. Wakefield." He paused. Then, "Ordinarily, I wouldn't, but Mr. Robertson felt that I should get in touch with you at once."

The other end squawked, nervously, I thought.

Stein thought so, too. "That's quite possible. However, Mr. Robertson feels that his time here in Washington is valuable. So valuable that he thinks that his business is soon going to call him back to Wisconsin Dells, if the merger referred to is delayed any longer. I beg your pardon?"

He twisted to throw me a wink over his shoulder as the telephone chattered frantically.

"That's exactly what I told Mr. Robertson... Yes, he knows of that... Yes, I have assured him that, in these days of business uncertainty and production difficulties, mergers are not as easily arranged as—" That Stein had a sense of humor when he wanted to use it.

"Is that right? I'm glad to hear it. One moment, while I check with Mr. Robertson." He held his hand over the mouthpiece and grinned at me. "They are ready to have a stroke. This man I'm talking to has no more authority than a jackrabbit, and he knows it. He wants to check with his boss, and call us back later. All right with you, Mr. Robertson?"

I laughed out loud, and he clamped the mouthpiece tighter. "I think so, Mr. W. W. Wakefield. As long as he puts the heat on that merger."

He went back on the telephone. "Mr. Robertson thinks he might be able to wait a trifle longer. He asked me to warn you, that as he is a very busy man, every minute of his time can cost a considerable amount of money and goods… Yes, I'll tell him that… I'll be waiting for your call… Yes, I will. Thank you, and good-bye." He hung up the telephone with a flourish.

"Satisfied, Mr. Robertson?"

I was satisfied. "Quite, Mr. W. W. Wakefield. Wouldst care for ein bier?"

Ein bier haben. He would.

The telephone rang about an hour later, and I answered it. It was the Old Man's voice.

"Mr. Robertson?" he said cautiously.

"Mr. Robertson speaking," I said. "Yes?"

"I'm calling," he told me in a voice that said he was annoyed, but didn't want to show it, "in reference to the Wisconsin Dells merger."

"Yes?" I gave him no help.

"You understand, Mr. Robertson, that such an important merger can hardly be arranged at a moment's notice."

Yes, I understood that. "But two days notice is more than sufficient, even allowing for an enormous amount of red tape." I put real regret into my voice. "It is not that I wouldn't like to let nature take its course, but other things must be taken into consideration." I hoped I sounded like the busy executive. "I believe that Mr. Wakefield, Mr. W. W. Wakefield, has explained that I am a very busy man, and that I can hardly be expected to wait indefinitely in even such a pleasant atmosphere."

The Old Man forced a cheery—and false—heartiness. "There are, or there might be, Mr. Robertson, other things that might induce you to stay. Many other things."

Threaten me, would he? "That, I doubt very much. I'm afraid I must insist—it's now two-twenty. If a merger, or at least a meeting cannot be arranged by tomorrow at the very latest, the reason for having a meeting will, for all practical purposes, have ceased to exist. Do I make myself clear?"

I certainly did. With a short-tempered bang, Smith hung up, after saying that he would call back later. I relayed the conversation to Bob Stein, and we sent down for lunch.

The Old Man called back about seven, when I was washing up, and Bob answered the telephone. By the time I came out he had all the information we needed, and was calling room service to clear the dishes.

"Meeting tonight," he said when he was finished. He was pleased with himself.

"Good." It was getting a little tiresome being cramped up. "When? Where?"

He shrugged. "Where? I couldn't say. Someone will call for us, somewhere between nine and ten. And," he added slowly, "it might be a good idea to wear the best bib and tucker, with Sunday School manners."

"Oh?" I said, "that kind of a party? Fine. I'm all ready now. Better get your hat."

At ten-thirty, the telephone rang. I answered it.

"This is the desk," it said. "Mr. Wakefield?"

"He's here," I said. "Wait a minute," and I passed the phone to Stein.

"Wakefield," he said. "Yes?"

The receiver chattered briefly.

"All right," and he waved at me. "Be right down." He turned. "Car waiting." It didn't take us long to get downstairs.

It was a sedan with a neat little drive-yourself tab on the right-hand door. Before we got near the car, Stein was careful to see who was the driver. He evidently was someone he knew, so Bob nodded curtly, and we got in and pulled away from the curb.

I DON'T know Washington at all, so I can't say where we made port. Not too far a drive, I imagine, if we had gone there directly. It was a good forty-five minutes before we ended our erratic turning of corners and sped up a long tree-bordered driveway.

"Nice place," I said to Stein as we braked to a stop in front of a long white-columned Southern portico. "Who lives here?"

He smiled and shook his head. "That's something I don't know. Does it matter?"

It didn't.

As we strode up the steps the Drive-Yourself pulled away, tires crackling on the white gravel. We both reached for the knocker at the same time, but before we had it, the door swung open. Stein recognized the young fellow who opened it and took our hats. A message passed between their eyes, and the young man almost imperceptibly shook his head in negation.

"Will you come this way, please?" and he led us down the hall.

The house was smaller than the outside had led me to expect. The builder had gone whole hog on the giant Greek columns and the wide sweep of the porch, and the inside of the house showed the results of the skimping. Not that it wasn't a far bigger and a far more expensive house than any average man would hope to have, but the limited space inside didn't go with those sweeping curves of the drive. I wondered who lived there.

The room where the doorman left us went with the inside of the house. So small it reminded me of the times when I tried to sell brushes during the depression, in Grosse Pointe, I expected every moment to have an underpaid maid, laundress, and butler come in to tell me that the lady of the house was out. In keeping with the faded appointments of the tiny room, a Chinese table held, for those who wait and read, an ancient collection of "Spur" and "Town and Country." As we sat and smoked, far off through the thin walls we could hear the soft rumble of voices. Occasionally a bass would rise above the sound, and a baritone would slide softly and soothingly across the pained roar. The front door opened and closed twice during the fifteen minutes or so we waited, and the footsteps that came in went past our room and pattered further down the hall. Each time, when the steps were out of reach of hearing, another door would open, and the distant voices would become almost distinguishable until the door again was shut. I looked curiously around the walls. Decorated with prints and pictures they were, yes, but with that faded permanency that to me spells the furnished house. The rugs were worn, worn to the shredding point, worn until the spurious Oriental design seemed an eerie Dali drawing. All it needed was the far-off smell of secondhand ham and cabbage.

The doorman slipped in and beckoned to us, a grim conspirator if ever I saw one. We followed him back to the entrance hall, back, back, to where the voices grew louder at every step. A double door—golden oak, or I don't know wood—barred the end of the hall, and the young fellow preceded us to throw it open with a semi-flourish. We walked in.

The place was blue with smoke. That was the first thing we saw. Lights there were in plenty, hanging around, hanging over the great oval table in the center of the room in a fiery glitter of glassy brilliants. The room was enormous, and I began to realize why this house was still in existence. Who cares about rugs if there is just one single room in the house where a ball or a party could be comfortably accommodated. Or a conference. I didn't know whose name appeared on the tax bills, but I would bet that it would be any other name besides the United States Government.

No group of men or women could produce that much smoke in a short time. That meeting had been going on for hours. As we stepped in through the double doors I tried to pick out anyone I knew, but the glare flickered in my eyes and I saw no face as more than just a pale blur against a background of tenuous blue. Tentatively I got inside the doors and they shut behind me with an abrupt finality. Two steps forward, three, four, five, and Stein drifted away from my side, away from the eyes that grew in size as I got closer to the table rim, toward the vacant chairs I saw slightly pulled away and ready for occupants. I stumbled over nothing and a reassuring hand touched mine. I felt callow, self-conscious, awkward. I never thought I'd be so glad to see Old Man Smith.

He stood alongside me as I sank gratefully into my ready chair. "Gentlemen," he announced quietly, "Mr. Peter A. Miller."

I half-bowed automatically, the proper thing to do, and the Old Man gave me his moral support by sitting next to me. He leaned over to say, "I won't introduce you formally. Point out who you want to know and I'll tell you who he is."

"Okay," I muttered, and felt in my pockets for cigarettes. I had to do something with my hands. I blew a cloud into the air and felt better. Settled back into the chair, I sent my glance around the table. Did I know anyone there?

At my right, the Old Man. His suit was wrinkled and his eyes were red-rimmed and tired. The large paper pad in front of him was covered with crisscross lines. On his right, a quite old man, bald and beetle-browed. His collar was open and wrinkled, his vest twisted under the lapel of his coat. I leaned toward Smith, and indicated his companion with my eyes.

"Morgan, Undersecretary of State," he said softly.

Morgan heard his name spoken, and shot a questioning glance my way. He realized what had been said and the beetlebrows slid upwards in a movement meant to be conciliatory. He bobbed his head with a cursory jerk and went back to staring across the table. I followed his glance.

The object of his affections seemed to be—yes, it was. Five-Star General Oliver P. Legree, not so affectionately called Simon by the men who served under him. I had been one of them. Trim and rigid and oh, so military he was, the very figure of a modern five-star general. His poker-stiff back thrust the tiers of ribbons to a sparkling glitter under the tinkling glare of the massive chandelier overhead. His face— well, it's been in enough rotogravures worldwide. The cigar was there, the big black cigar he never lit and never lost. His trademark was that cigar; his trademark was that and his jutting jaw that to everyone but his compatriots spelled determination and grit. To his staff and his men—me—it meant an ill-fitting lower plate.

That prognathous jaw was tilted, aimed at Morgan, and Morgan knew it. What had gone on just before I had come in? Just as I started to turn my glance away, the General threw his famous scowl directly at me. For one long second our eyes clung, almost glared. Then, without a sign of emotion or recognition he went back to staring at the Undersecretary with an intensity almost violent. Shaken back into self-consciousness by that grim stare I tried to fit together some of the other faces about the table.

Admiral Mason-Nason-Lacey—Admiral Lacey. I'd met him just a few days before, in that ill-fated conference in the White House. What was the other name? Jessop. He was there, too, alongside Lacey. But where was the Army, outside of Simon Legree? That was like Simon, at that. Let the Navy stick together; Legree was the *General*, and as such was himself the Army.

Who were the others? I knew none of them, certainly, although some trick of memory made me sure that I had seen or heard of them before. Like faces in an old school album they presented themselves to me, and for a long fraction of a minute I delved deep, trying to recall. A voice, that deep barking bass I had heard while waiting, boomed across the table.

"Mr. Morgan!" and the table seemed to quiver. "Mr. Morgan!" and the tenseness seemed to flow back into that huge room like a warm current. The Old Man leaned over and answered my unspoken question.

"Senator Suggs, Foreign Affairs Chairman."

I eyed the redoubtable senator. Short, swarthy skin that belied all his ranted racial theories, hair that straggled by intent over his weak green eyes, and a chin that retreated and quivered and joggled in time with his twitching adolescent eyebrows. Six solid terms in the Senate; six solid terms of appealing to the highest in theory and the lowest in fact; six terms of seniority for the chairmanship of committees far too important for a bigot; six terms of Suggs, Suggs, Suggs. The bass rumbled on.

"We're no further ahead, Morgan, than we were two hours ago. This, definitely cannot go on, if it has to be taken to the people themselves."

Morgan pondered well before he answered, and the room stilled.

"Senator," he said at last; "this is right now in the hands of the people, if you consider that you are one of the elected representatives, and the rest of us are chosen, with one exception, by those same elected representatives. The exception, naturally, is Mr. Miller."

Five Star Simon snorted. His nasal voice carried well. "People?" and that brittle snap was only too familiar to me.

"What have the people to do with it? This is no time for anything but a decision, and a quick one!"

Morgan agreed with that. "Correct, General. The question, I believe, is not that a decision be made, but the wording and definition of that decision."

"Bah!" and the cigar jumped to the other side. "Words! Definitions! Decisions! Words, words, words! Let's decide what's to be done and do it!"

The Undersecretary coughed gently behind his palm. "Unfortunately, General Legree, for the sake of speedy action, and as unfortunately for the sake of all concerned, words mean one thing to one man, and another thing to a second."

A FINE party this turned out to be. In the dark as to what happened before I came in, and equally at sea as to what was going on, I leaned toward the Old Man.

"What's this?" I whispered.

He shot a quick retort. "Keep your mouth shut for the time being." He paused, and then bent in my direction. "You'll get your chance to talk." He grasped my extended arm tightly. "I'll nudge you when the time comes. Then talk, and *talk*! You know what I mean?"

Did I? I didn't know. He saw my indecision and motioned for quiet. Evidently he was expecting me to catch the trend if I waited long enough. I waited, and I watched, and I listened.

Simon had been right about one thing. Words, words, words. But I began to get some of the drift. They'd already settled the part of the problem I thought was supposed to be bothering them. They'd decided that since the news on me was out, the facts had to be faced—the way they understand facing them.

I should have been reading the papers or listening to the radio. It must have been something to hear when the news that I was a new secret weapon to end them all was confirmed; but they'd confused the issue by indicating that I was just one of the men with the new power, and that the country was now practically blanketed with it.

It was fine for them. It meant that the people were happy, and that Army, Navy and all the other departments were being openly and publicly adulated for the fine thing they had done for everyone.

The Undersecretary made an answer to one of Simon's remarks. I hadn't been listening for a few seconds while the scheme sank in, but this registered.

"You're right, of course, General. Certain foreign information bureaus won't be deceived by the confusion we've created. And that still leaves us with the unfortunate need for speedy action on the case of Mr. Miller."

Suggs rolled his bass across the room. It was the only characteristic he had favorable to eye or ear.

"Unfortunate, Mr. Undersecretary? Unfortunate is hardly the word to describe an event so favorable for the fortunes for all."

Favorable. Me? Was I good or bad? I came in just in the middle of the picture. Keep your ears and your eyes and your ears open, Miller, and catch up on the feature attraction.

Suggs licked his razor-sharp lips and hooked his fingers in his stained vest.

"'Unfortunate,' Mr. Undersecretary? Hardly!" He loved to hear his own voice. "This country, these great United States, these states have never in their existence been in such a favorable position as today..."

I would rather have read the Congressional Record. That, at least, I could have discarded when I became bored.

"No, never in such a favorable position; diplomatically, economically…"

The Undersecretary coughed politely. It's nice to be tactful and know how to break in.

"To use your own words, Senator. 'Hardly!' Diplomatically we are at the brink of one of the worst imaginable pitfalls."

The medals on Five Star clinked. "Bosh!"

Morgan went on. "Where would you like to live, gentlemen?" and his glance flicked around the table; "in the best liked or most hated country in the world?"

It mattered not to Five Star, nor to Suggs.

"What difference does it make, Mr. Undersecretary? Speaking for myself and my constituents, I can truthfully say that the opinion of the world matters not one good solitary damn. Who cares what some other country has got to say, if words can't be backed up with action? Right now, and you know it as well as you're sitting there, Mr. Undersecretary, right now Uncle Sam is known all over the world as Uncle Sucker, and Uncle Shylock. Europe and Asia have had what they wanted over my protests and those of my constituents, and now Europe and Asia can go hang, for all I care. That's What they want us to do!"

He gave Morgan no chance to break in. That rolling bass rattled off the walls and crinkled my ears.

"Europe and Asia and the rest of the world could never affect us one way or another, favorable or otherwise, if it weren't for the ninny-headed mouthings of a few influential morons. Fight, Mr. Undersecretary, fight and murder and declare war and blow up millions of people and then run to Uncle Sam to pay the bills. I say, Mr. Undersecretary, I say what I've said before and what I'll say again; if Europe and Asia and the rest of the world don't like what we do here in these United States, let Europe and Asia and the rest of the world go to hell!"

Suggs wasn't a bit excited. Those grand, those mellifluous and rotund phrases rolled out of those skinny lips at a mile-a-minute pace with never a flicker of emotion but a nervous twitching of the drooping eyelids. If that was the way he talked when calm, I could see why he had been sent back and back to the Senate time after time.

The General deliberately tossed his cigar on the floor and pounded his fist on the table.

"Well said, Senator! My sentiments exactly. If Europe and Asia and the rest of the world don't like what we do here, let 'em all go to hell, or better yet, let's send them there in a hand-basket."

Bloodthirsty old bat. I never remembered seeing him any too close to the jumping-off point. That's what generals are for, they tell me.

"I say to hell with them all, and the sooner they know about it, the better for all concerned." His gaudy gold case, the gift of a grateful staff, was on the table in front of him, and he jerked out a cigar with a flourish. A light with a gold lighter, and he puffed thick clouds.

Morgan coughed politely. "Regardless, Senator, of what has or what is happening, we're concerned at present with what might happen."

Suggs opened his mouth like a thirsty carp and closed it again as Morgan went on.

"Call it what you like, Senator; General Legree will agree with me that this perfect defense—if defense is the word—is equally well the perfect weapon. Right, General?"

Legree pursed pontifical lips for a reply and was annoyed when Morgan paused only momentarily.

"Perfect defense means the nullification of an opposing weapon. Obviously, a weaponless army is no longer anything but a disciplined mob. In correlation, Senator, *our* arms and weapons are still effective, and—you mentioned the distrust (or dislike, or hatred, or whatever you will) held for us by Europe and Asia. Now, Senator, think of yourself and your constituents: is it not far better that Europe and Asia and the world be solaced and comforted by the announcement that we would use our...Iron Curtain only in our own defense? Would it not be better—how many years, Senator, have there been recorded of universal peace? How many years?"

Some men can sit poker-stiff, yet give the impression of teetering slowly on their heels, slowly counting the horses' teeth. Suggs was a horse trader from away back.

He said, "Mr. Morgan, I say I can appreciate your viewpoint. I can even appreciate the fact that you mean exactly what you say. But—!"

Sharks must have teeth like that; broken and yellow, and razor-keen. The smile of the Senator fascinated me.

"But—! Mr. Undersecretary, who's been doing all the fighting, and who's been starting all these wars? The United States? No, sir! We just get in them too late to do anything but pay all the bills!" He leaned forward and fixed the tabletop with a piscine stare.

"Look at it this way, the only way. When this whats-his-name dies, all these countries look at the map and start mobilizing the Guards. How do we know how long he's going to live, or how long he's going to keep this magic head of his?"

My magic head itched, and I rubbed it.

"Now, here's what I've said before, and here's what I say now—we can't let the world get away with murder—'murder' is what I said, Mr. Undersecretary, and 'murder' is what I mean. Didn't you say—now, tell us the truth, now—haven't you always said that it would be just a question of time until just about anyone has the secret of the atomic bomb? Didn't you say that?"

Morgan nodded. "Quite often I've said that, Senator. Too often for some."

Suggs was triumphant. "All right, now. You've hung yourself on your own rope and you don't know it. Answer me this; now, what's to prevent anyone who has the bomb from coming over here and using it on us? What's to prevent them?"

They had been all through that before, and Morgan knew it was no use to answer.

Suggs was his own echo. "Nothing's to prevent them, not a thing in the world. How many times have I come right out and said in public that the only way to keep the world where we want it is to just make sure that no one else is going to get it? How many times?"

Morgan rubbed his cigarette in the ashtray and spoke to the table. "You've said that many times, Senator. That's true, too true. I, on the other hand, have asked you many times if you've thought that the only way to make sure no other nation gets the bomb would be to go right in and make *sure*. You agreed with me that *that* would mean force. Force, meaning war. Right, Senator?"

And the Senator, champion of Man and Humanity and Right said, "Right, Mr. Undersecretary. Right. We have the bomb, haven't we?"

Morgan didn't say much in answer to that. I don't think there was much he could find to say. Psychologists claim there is hardly anyone, anyone with a modicum of logic in a brain-pan, who cannot eventually see the light of reason. Maybe. Maybe calm logic could force Senator Suggs and his brain-pan off his muddy detour. Maybe humanity and decency and all the other things that complement the civilized man to this day lie submerged in that pithecanthropic skull. Maybe, but I hated his guts then, and I do now.

I cleared my throat, and it must have been louder than I thought, because all the eyes swung my way. Well, so what? If I had anything at all to say about what was going to happen, or if I was ever going to be more than just a rubber stamp, now was the time to find out. After all, I'd been asked to bring my harp to the party, and I was going to play.

So I said, "Senator. Senator Suggs!"

He was a little taken aback. Like having the sweeper talk back.

"Senator," I said, "you talk big. Let's get right down to rock-bottom, and let's stay there until we're finished. Okay?... All right; in words of one syllable, you want us to do what amounts to declaring war on the rest of the world, winning the war and then running things our way. Right?"

The Senator teetered on those mental heels again. His lips sucked in and sharp hollows formed in his cheeks. I could see his mind reach all the way across the table and throw face-up the cards, one by one.

"You're Mr. Miller, I presume, although we haven't been formally introduced." His eager eyes flickered over me. "You haven't said much so far, and it's just as well that you spoke when you did."

Legree groped for his cigar case, and Suggs rumbled on.

"You said I talk big, Mr. Miller, and I'm going to take that as a compliment. Yes, I do talk big. And you talk plain. I like men who talk plain. We're going to get along well together." And he paused to let his thoughts catch up.

I gave my needle a little push. "You're still talking big, Senator," I reminded him.

He resented that, and tried to hide it. "Hardly, Mr. Miller. Hardly. But you asked a question, and I'll try to talk plain, like you do. If we have to fight the rest of the world to do things our way, the American way, then my answer is yes. Yes!"

Legree grinned his saturnine smile through a blue wreath of smoke and Morgan sat back in his chair with an almost silent exhalation. The rest of the group seated around that great table affected me hardly at all one way or another. Suggs was the spokesman for one faction and I—well, Morgan was willing to let me talk; the Old Man was sunk in the dumb obscurity of his chair, and who else was there to speak for me? Who else?

All right, Miller. Take it slow and easy. Watch your temper. Say what you have that's important, and let it go at that. But—say it!

Now, there's one thing I learned long ago; you get a lot further if the other loses his temper first, and the best way to pry the lid of a temper is the use of the unexpected. The man who is handy with his hands will crack wide open with ridicule, with words used as the lever. The man who is handy with words is a different nut to crack; slap him down with insults while his verbal guard is down. If his temper doesn't snap in the first two minutes, it never will.

So, because I thought it was the right thing to say, and because I didn't like the Senator anyway, I said, "Senator Suggs, you talked plain. That's good. I like men who talk plain. Let's have some more of that talk. Let's get this right on the record for everyone here to see and hear.

"I don't like you, Senator. I like neither you nor your ideas, nor anything about you or your thoughts. How long has it been, Senator, since anyone has told you right to your face—not in a newspaper—that you're a self-convinced liar and a hypocrite, and that you and your ideas and everything about you stink to high heaven?"

"Stink" was the word that got him. He'd expected a nice gentlemanly quarrel with gentlemanly words above the table and rapiers below, and instead had walked around the corner and taken a barrel-stave across the mouth. His face flushed in an instant to a livid unhealthy red, his lips pulled away from his yellow teeth, his eyes seemed to protrude visibly. A beautiful sight.

It took him long seconds to throttle his gasping shock. I gave him just enough time to inhale for a long tirade, just long enough to open that fish-like mouth for words that might have been anything, then I let him have it again. And I don't know whether or not I told you, I was a sergeant before I got busted back to private, first class.

"Shut up!" I bellowed, and my roar boomed back at me from all those startled, those stunned faces. Shut up shut up shut up shut up...

I'M CERTAIN that those walls had never heard anything above a quiet murmur before that night. I just shocked Suggs and the rest into a panicky silence while I ranted. I had to talk fast, because while volume and violence are a good temporary substitute for brilliance, I knew I wasn't going to have the floor forever.

"Let's talk straight, Suggs. Get this once, because I'm not repeating it, and get that silly look off your face..." I'd heard he was vain. "...you and your constituents and your Army and your Navy can go to hell, as far as I care for any of them. I'm the man you want to keep your shirt clean while the rest of the world wallows in filth; I'm the man that's supposed to let you and your type, God forbid, rule the world; I'm the man—" I leaned over the table as far as I could, as far as I dared.

"Suggs," and I poured venom down his shirtfront, "the only thing that keeps me from despising the Government of the United States and the people in it is the fact that I know you're not typical. You're a freak, a monster!" And I threw in another to keep him off balance. "You even *look* like a fish!

"Remember this, Senator. Remember this one thing; if I ever see, if I ever hear as much as one word from you about war or bombs, in private or public, you'll live just long enough for me to hear about it!"

I threw a disgusted glance at the rest of the table. "One thing you don't know, Senator, is that I can kill you where you sit. Smith!"

The Old Man was astonished as the Senator, who sat with gaping piscine mouth and pop eyes. "Yes, Peter?"

"Tell him," I snapped. "Tell him how Kellner found out that I can stop a heart just as fast as I can a truck. And you'd better tell him while you're at it that Kellner thinks I'm emotionally unstable, subject to fits of temper. Tell that to the Senator. Tell him what Kellner said about me."

Smith coughed. "I think you all agree that Mr. Miller is a trifle upset. You can form your own opinion as to his temper. As to the other...well, Dr. Kellner is the top man in his field. He tested Peter—Mr. Miller—very thoroughly. I would give very careful consideration to whatever he says about Peter's capabilities."

Now you can see what makes a diplomat. When Smith was finished talking it sounded as though Kellner had actually said that I could murder someone. And yet Smith hadn't told even a tiny bit of a lie. Lying, as any married man knows, is knowing what to say and what not to say at the right time. But to get back to the rest. I dismissed Suggs. I ignored him for all the rest of the time he was there. Even when I looked directly at him, and that hurt him. I have hopes, high hopes, that might have brought on the real heart attack he had the next day.

"So," I said generally to the rest of the table, "let's just assume from now on that you're dealing with a homicidal maniac with unlimited power. Is that the phrase you were thinking of, General?"

General Legree jumped as though he had seen me pull the pin on a live grenade.

"Forget it, General," I told him kindly. "I just read a lot of your speeches. Now you, Mr. Morgan, you're apparently having a meeting. I got here a little late. How about telling me the score?"

The tension seemed to seep out of the room as tangible as a stream of water. Suggs shrank up in his chair like a little old kobold, the Generals shifted into easier positions with the old familiar creak of expensive leather, and the man Smith looked right at me with his right eye closed. I'd said what he wanted me to say, but now what? Where did we go from here?

Undersecretary of State Theodore Morgan was one of the career men to be found in State Departments throughout the world, if by that you mean someone who has had the same job for years. The newspapers liked to tee off on him occasionally, using his pseudo-British mannerisms and habits for caricature. And the great American public, I suppose, considered him pretty much as a jerk, as the public is most apt to do when regarding a man who wore striped pants and a top hat in public and apparently liked it. But the Old Man, Smith—and I never did find out if Morgan was Smith's boss or vice versa—set me straight on a lot of things about Morgan. He had a fairly rough job, as jobs are when you do something you dislike merely because policy has been set by higher-ups. Let's just say he did the best he could, and let it go at that.

He was in charge of the meeting, all right. He knew just how to handle Simon Legree, and without Suggs things went fairly smooth—on the surface.

"Mr. Miller," he said, "you made a rather abrupt entrance into the conversation. I think it better if we have it understood right now that we prefer to use reason instead of volume."

"Call me Pete," I said. I knew, somehow that he hadn't disapproved too much of what I'd said, and he was cracking down at the outset just to show the rest that *he* wasn't intimidated. "Pete is all right with me, since I'm sure that this is all among friends." I looked around, and they were all friends. Especially the two generals that had seen me stop the trucks from the Federal Building window. I don't say they were actually afraid; just cautious. Just friends.

I went on. "Maybe I can help break the ice. I suppose you were talking about what you were going to do about things in general, and in particular, me. Well, go ahead."

So they did.

I won't bother with the details of the rest of the meeting or conference, or whatever you want to call it, because I don't think the details are too important. For one thing, when the first flush wore off, and I began to realize the colossal bluff I'd gotten away with, I got a little weak in the knees. For another, Morgan and Smith did all the talking to amount to anything. Legree, who seemed to be the self-appointed spokesman for the Army, really didn't have much to say when he knew that the State Department had all the cards, with me the joker. The Navy played right along when it was tentatively agreed that it was to be an island where I would be "stationed," as they euphemistically called it; they knew that islands are surrounded by water, and who sails on the water? The FBI got in their little piece when they were made responsible for general security. My contribution was that I was to be responsible to State, in the person of Smith, and Smith was to be the boss as far as conditions were concerned. When I brought that up I knew the Old Man was thinking of all the times I'd complained about his guardianship, and wrote him a tiny note so he wouldn't get too pleased with himself.

"The lesser—or the least—of many evils. Don't get swell-headed." He just grinned when he read it, and stuck it in his pocket to save for Morgan, I feel sure.

Smith and Bob Stein and I were the last to leave, and Morgan's grip for an old man was firm as we shook hands. "You did an excellent demolition job on the Senator," he said. "You know, Pete, there is one of the few people that have made me regret the job I have."

"Forget it," I told him. "You can get fired. Me, I got seniority in a lifetime job. As far as that carp is concerned, you can consider me your chief steward. I'll run ten miles to take up your grievance with Suggs."

Morgan smiled politely as he ushered us to the door, but I don't think he knew what I meant. They don't have unions in State.

THE ISLAND isn't too bad. I swore, years ago, with the first cold I ever remember having, that I would never care if I ever saw snow again. And where I am, there isn't any snow. The beach is yellow as gold, the sun comes up every day in the east and sets in the west, and I've got for my personal use the biggest, shiniest bar you ever saw in all your life. They ship in draft beer for me all the way from La Crosse, Wisconsin, and Munich, Germany. Every month I get a four-quart keg from Belfast in Ireland, and I've got all the gadgets I need to mix anything a barkeep could dream up. The ice I get from what probably is a six-hundred dollar refrigerator that makes nothing but ice cubes. I have a subscription to practically every magazine I ever heard of, and I get daily aerial delivery—that's right. A little Piper Cub with floats drops the New York *Times*, the *Monitor*, and a couple of others every morning—of the newspapers with the least amount of junk. I used to get the Detroit papers, but I found out it took too much mental effort to avoid looking at the Vital Statistics, where they record the marriages and deaths.

I finally learned to play bridge. Euchre doesn't seem the same without a barful of people, and pinochle is not the game that Stein is good at. Bob Stein, the poor guy—although he never says one word about it—takes everything in his stride. He spends six weeks out of every eight here with me and the others that form the crew of this little island afloat in the Southern Sea. Food's good, and with no limit to variety and type. We can't be too far from somewhere, because every once in a while we hear a rattle and banging somewhere out to sea. Once we heard what sounded like a full scale battle. I pried it out of Bob Stein that it was just maneuvers, as he called it. I know better. I see nothing but naval craft, and I suspect that they're not always just at the horizon for practice.

National affairs? Well, they're not too bad. The big noise came when the UN wanted my custody and didn't get it. The Old Man once asked me why I wasn't in favor of it, and I told him. In theory, yes; in practice, the UN was too dangerous. Personally, I felt that I could trust very few, and none that I hadn't known before all this happened. UN supervision meant that I would serve too many masters, and that I didn't like. And too, there are too many people in the United States that don't believe in the UN, and might be tempted to do something about it if they thought I owed allegiance to someone else besides the United States. I couldn't stir up anything like that, I told him. Deep down in my heart, I wanted people to like me, to admire me, to think that I was their hero, and no other country's. I think I can see admiration and affection in the eyes of the civilians and sailors that supply me the food and the other things I ask for. They ask me every once in a while if I'm all right, if I need women. I tell them I don't, that I'm reconciled with living like I am. And that's true; I want no other woman except Helen, and her I can't have, for devious reasons; my name is just anonymous to the world. Smith talked me into that—his idea was that if no one knew who I was, I'd be just that much harder to find. He explained that there are several other islands set up the same as mine, with almost the same conditions and the same surroundings. He calls it camouflage on a grand scale, and he's the boss. I know I'm not very smart; just smart enough to know that the reports in the *Times* about other people in other parts of the world with my capabilities are some of the grand-scale camouflage started by Smith's agents. I'm all alone, and I know it. But sometimes I wake up in the middle of the night and go for a walk along the beach and kick up a little sand with my bare feet like Helen and I did on our honeymoon. They asked me once if I really had to do that. I told them I felt like it, and they asked me why. I didn't tell them I was just lonesome.

CONFIDENTIAL MEMO
FROM: Morgan
TO: Smith

MESSAGE: I don't care how many plants got hit. Draft another plant. Draft the Times itself. But get those special editions to Miller and get them there today. Repeat, today! You're already one day late in getting started on those hints of probable attack. Better rush the softening up. The way things are going, all plans are off, and we may need him in a hurry. And that means we'll need cooperation. You know Miller. You saw those reports on the Suggs post-mortem. Do I have to draw diagrams for you? You've got unlimited authority. Use it. I'm serious about drafting the Times if you have to. **But GET THOSE PAPERS PRINTED AND GET THEM TO HIM TODAY...**

THE END

If you've enjoyed this book, you will not want to miss these terrific titles...

If you've enjoyed this book, you will not want to miss these terrific titles…

ARMCHAIR SCI-FI, FANTASY, & HORROR DOUBLE NOVELS, $12.95 each

D-21   **EMPIRE OF EVIL** by Robert Arnette
THE SIGN OF THE TIGER by Alan E. Nourse & J. A. Meyer

D-22   **OPERATION SQUARE PEG** by Frank Belknap Long
ENCHANTRESS OF VENUS by Leigh Brackett

D-23   **THE LIFE WATCH** by Lester Del Rey
CREATURES OF THE ABYSS by Murray Leinster

D-24   **LEGION OF LAZARUS** by Edmond Hamilton
STAR HUNTER by Andre Norton

D-25   **EMPIRE OF WOMEN** by John Fletcher
ONE OF OUR CITIES IS MISSING by Irving Cox

D-26   **THE WRONG SIDE OF PARADISE** by Raymond F. Jones
THE INVOLUNTARY IMMORTALS by Rog Phillips

D-27   **EARTH QUARTER** by Damon Knight
ENVOY TO NEW WORLDS by Keith Laumer

D-28   **SLAVES TO THE METAL HORDE** by Milton Lesser
HUNTERS OUT OF TIME by Joseph E. Kelleam

D-29   **RX JUPITER SAVE US** by Ward Moore
BEWARE THE USURPERS by Geoff St. Reynard

D-30   **SECRET OF THE SERPENT** by Don Wilcox
CRUSADE ACROSS THE VOID by Dwight V. Swain

ARMCHAIR SCIENCE FICTION CLASSICS, $12.95 each

C-7   **THE SHAVER MYSTERY, Book One**
by Richard S. Shaver

C-8   **THE SHAVER MYSTERY, Book Two**
by Richard S. Shaver

C-9   **MURDER IN SPACE** by David V. Reed
by David V. Reed

ARMCHAIR MASTERS OF SCIENCE FICTION SERIES, $16.95 each

M-3   **MASTERS OF SCIENCE FICTION, Vol. Three**
Robert Sheckley, "The Perfect Woman" and other tales

M-4   **MASTERS OF SCIENCE FICTION, Vol. Four**
Mack Reynolds, "Stowaway" and other tales

If you've enjoyed this book, you will not want to miss these terrific titles...

ARMCHAIR SCI-FI & HORROR DOUBLE NOVELS, $12.95 each

D-51 **A GOD NAMED SMITH** by Henry Slesar
WORLDS OF THE IMPERIUM by Keith Laumer

D-52 **CRAIG'S BOOK** by Don Wilcox
EDGE OF THE KNIFE by H. Beam Piper

D-53 **THE SHINING CITY** by Rena M. Vale
THE RED PLANET by Russ Winterbotham

D-54 **THE MAN WHO LIVED TWICE** by Rog Phillips
VALLEY OF THE CROEN by Lee Tarbell

D-55 **OPERATION DISASTER** by Milton Lesser
LAND OF THE DAMNED by Berkeley Livingston

D-56 **CAPTIVE OF THE CENTAURIANESS** by Poul Anderson
A PRINCESS OF MARS by Edgar Rice Burroughs

D-57 **THE NON-STATISTICAL MAN** by Raymond F. Jones
MISSION FROM MARS by Rick Conroy

D-58 **INTRUDERS FROM THE STARS** by Ross Rocklynne
FLIGHT OF THE STARLING by Chester S. Geier

D-59 **COSMIC SABOTEUR** by Frank M. Robinson
LOOK TO THE STARS by Willard Hawkins

D-60 **THE MOON IS HELL!** by John W. Campbell, Jr.
THE GREEN WORLD by Hal Clement

ARMCHAIR SCIENCE FICTION CLASSICS, $12.95 each

C-16 **THE SHAVER MYSTERY, Book Three**
by Richard S. Shaver

C-17 **THE PLANET STRAPPERS**
by Raymond Z. Gallun

C-18 **THE FOURTH "R"**
by George O. Smith

ARMCHAIR SCIENCE FICTION & HORROR GEMS SERIES, $12.95 each

G-5 **SCIENCE FICTION GEMS, Vol. Three**
C. M. Kornbluth and others

G-6 **HORROR GEMS, Vol. Three**
August Derleth and others

If you've enjoyed this book, you will not want to miss these terrific titles...

ARMCHAIR SCI-FI & HORROR DOUBLE NOVELS, $12.95 each

D-71   **THE DEEP END** by Gregory Luce
TO WATCH BY NIGHT by Robert Moore Williams

D-72   **SWORDSMAN OF LOST TERRA** by Poul Anderson
PLANET OF GHOSTS by David V. Reed

D-73   **MOON OF BATTLE** by J. J. Allerton
THE MUTANT WEAPON by Murray Leinster

D-74   **OLD SPACEMEN NEVER DIE!** John Jakes
RETURN TO EARTH by Bryan Berry

D-75   **THE THING FROM UNDERNEATH** by Milton Lesser
OPERATION INTERSTELLAR by George O. Smith

D-76   **THE BURNING WORLD** by Algis Budrys
FOREVER IS TOO LONG by Chester S. Geier

D-77   **THE COSMIC JUNKMAN** by Rog Phillips
THE ULTIMATE WEAPON by John W. Campbell

D-78   **THE TIES OF EARTH** by James H. Schmitz
CUE FOR QUIET by Thomas L. Sherred

D-79   **SECRET OF THE MARTIANS** by Paul W. Fairman
THE VARIABLE MAN by Philip K. Dick

D-80   **THE GREEN GIRL** by Jack Williamson
THE ROBOT PERIL by Don Wilcox

ARMCHAIR SCIENCE FICTION CLASSICS, $12.95 each

C-25   **THE STAR KINGS**
by Edmond Hamilton

C-26   **NOT IN SOLITUDE**
by Kenneth Gantz

C-32   **PROMETHEUS II**
by S. J. Byrne

ARMCHAIR SCIENCE FICTION & HORROR GEMS SERIES, $12.95 each

G-7   **SCIENCE FICTION GEMS, Vol. Seven**
Jack Sharkey and others

G-8   **HORROR GEMS, Vol. Eight**
Seabury Quinn and others